The Cat's Eyes

K.A.McKeown

Copyright © 2017 by K.A.McKeown

All rights reserved. This book or any portion thereof may not be reproduced or used in any manner whatsoever without the express written permission of the author except for the use of brief quotations in a book review.

This is a work of fiction. Names, characters, businesses, places, events and incidents are either the products of the author's imagination or used in a fictitious manner. Any resemblance to actual persons, living or dead, or actual events is purely coincidental

If you would like to contact the author, please visit www.kamckeown.com, email K.A.McKeown@outlook.com or find me on twitter @K_A_Mckeown.

To the person who, if ever I were to be asked what I would want to do today if it were my last, my response would be to go to the beach and skim stones with them. To my best friend, my soul mate and the person who brought true happiness in to my life; my wife, Jo.

Thank you for everything, you are wonderful!

(Oh, and of course Cara, our naughty tortie, because she's full of so much… character)

Contents

1. Beasts, Fears and Dreams
2. Whale Watching
3. Walking the Hood
4. Hard Work, Hurt and Heartache
5. Money Matters
6. Perceptions and realities
7. Frustrations, Fortunes and Fun
8. Laughter, Loneliness and Life
9. Death Dues
10. Dreams, Escapes and Realities
11. Colours of Life
12. A New Beginning
13. Heroine in the Park
14. Goodbyes and Tears
15. Fireworks and Futures
16. Lachrymosity and Promises
17. Chance Encounters
18. Peripeteia Al Fresco
19. Faded Grandeur
20. Round and Round and Round We Go
21. Life Goes On

Beasts, Fears and Dreams

Mmm, perfect! Just lying here, alone for once, basking in the warmth of the spring sunshine with the heat caressing my toned athletic body as I lounge on a bed of soft downy cushions. I shouldn't be lying on them like this really, but hey, you have to indulge yourself every now and again and get lost in the moment. Enjoying life is what I am made for.

Indulgently, I extend my powerful limbs, enjoying the sensation of muscles stretching in the warmth of the day and feeling the softness of the cushions. I must sustain this mighty body of mine and have ensured I have enough fine food and drink by my side to satisfy my needs after I have fully rested; everything is purrrrfect. I deserve this life and know I have earned this moment, I am worth it. Warm reddish rays of light pass through my closed eyelids as I relax, my breathing slows and I can feel my heart rate calming too. Perhaps I should have a quick cheeky nap, it would seem a waste not to make the most of this moment of tranquility in my otherwise hectic life.

Tap, tap, tap.

What the hell is that noise and where the hell is it coming from? How bloody annoying, I wish it would just sod off, I can't believe my luck, something's spoiling the first moment I have had all day for some sodding solitude and silence! I feel my anger rising, I feel the tranquility of the moment slipping from my fragile grasp and am desperate to cling to it like a life raft in stormy seas, I need to cling on for dear life and try to relax. I will ignore it, I am sure it will stop, I deserve this moment of luxury.

Tap, tap, tap.

No, no, NO! This isn't right; sod off, let me have just a little more peace in the sun. Everything was going so well, I've finally got some peace, started to relax after a full day's exertions and had a light bite to let me settle. Mmmm, the mackerel was so bloody delicious, best I have had in ages, well since this morning anyways. I can feel the raft slipping away from me now and feel powerless to control the situation, which is a rarity, and I hate that. Hate and anger are never good relaxation buddies and the thought doesn't help me settle. I make one final attempt to relax and get back on track. Sod off and let me sleep!

Tap, tap, tap.

Suddenly, I sense a presence, and instantly I know that something is wrong, very wrong. Seconds later, I can hear scraping — a long, slow, nails-on-a-chalkboard type screeching, it is eery, loud, threatening and... close. My eyes reluctantly prise open and I am on alert, the dream has gone and is forgotten, melted away like the early mist on a summer's morning. The soft glow from a streetlight lazily glows through the half closed blinds to create puddles of soft light in an otherwise dark room. There is a certain chill in the air that only seems to exist at this time of night, when the warmth of life is held under the soft duvets and blankets keeping slumbering people encased in their soft caressing dreams. All is quiet, all apart from the scraping noise, quieter now, but still there. Slow, menacing and… even closer. Hairs rise, pulse quickens and muscles tense, my senses are on full alert now. This isn't right, no-one and nothing should be here, it is the middle of the night and everyone is sleeping, or should be.

The illusion of safety and security vanish. I was foolish to succumb to slumber so easily, I should have been more alert, only fools let their guard down. I stretch my limbs ever so slowly to get the blood flowing, no sudden movements, just silent and steady, preparing for freeze, fight or flight depending on what has snuck its way into my presence; someone or something is here, in my sanctuary. No! Without lifting my head, I know my fears are real. I see something move, slow and stealthy, on the periphery of my vision. Fur, black sinister fur that blends with the night. This isn't a person, this is a *thing*, a predator, an animal hunter here in my world, my safe world, in the dead of night. Shadows flicker, ever so slightly as the thing stealthily moves from the side of the window in to the darkest recess of the terrace, watching, waiting. I can feel its presence, the aura of evil is almost overpowering. I know without doubt that I am its focus and it is stalking me now, I can feel it watching, moving, threatening, looking for a weakness in the defences, looking for a way to attack me when I am at my most vulnerable.

What to do? I can't think straight, sleepiness and fear are not the best ingredients for clarity of thought. Fein sleep, close my eyes and pretend it isn't here? It may move on and find some other prey, someone else who unfortunately falls into this beast's path to fall foul of its violence and hate. No, I know it is coming for *me*, it has sought me out and I am its sole target and focus, it can sense my fear and it is just waiting for the right moment to strike, hoping to find an easy way in to my one and only sanctuary. My world isn't safe anymore, how did this happen, what did I do, what can I do? Freezing and ignoring isn't an option; fight or flight then? Deep down, I know I have nowhere to run now, it is too late, there is nowhere I can hide - I am trapped in this bloody room. What moments before had been my cosy safe sanctuary is now my prison. Oh, how cruel is life, I may as well be tied to a sacrificial altar just to make things even easier for this killer, would that make things better if I were? It might be hunting me, or it might be looking for the opportunity to fight a worthy opponent, hoping for the thrill of violence, living for orgasmic like joy of conflict, tasting blood, feasting on fear and ripped flesh. No, flight isn't an option, the executioner knows its business, if I run, I know I would soon feel its teeth sinking into the back of my neck, sinking into my once perfect body, its stinking rank breath and look of triumph in its demon-like eyes the last things I will smell and see in this once seemingly beautiful and safe world. I now realise how safety is just a fleeting illusion for the weak and small minded.

I must fight. Fight for my life. Fight this demon, this beast that by chance or design has sought me out and found me when I am at my most exposed — naked, sleep weary, in the dead of night, having foolishly relaxed and dreamt of better times I had thought were still to come. Decision made, I feel stronger and more empowered. I decide I must take the initiative. I can feel my powerful limbs waking, blood now flowing, muscles charging and readying for what must be. I listen, the scraping has finally ceased and I know it has stopped and is watching me. It has sensed my alertness, my awareness of its menacing presence. It knows, it waits, it has no fear, just the blood lust.

With one last small and final stretch, I am ready. My senses are fully alert now, time slows down and I am and prepared. I am resigned that violence is the only course of action open to me, it will be a fight, to the death. Slowly, ever so slowly, I raise my head by the smallest fraction, just enough to increase my field of vision, and take one last look before I will act Any slight advantage I can give myself, however small, might make the difference between life and death for me. My eyes raise to the darkness and eyes filled with fury and hate stare back, it is already watching me, knowing it has found its prey, violence shining from them like sunlit diamonds. I shudder, I am looking at evilness personified, I am looking at my death.

My courage wavers and my eyes lower, I haven't fully committed, I can still consider my options — it might go away. Sadly, I know this is the moment, this is my moment, or more likely it is the beast's moment, the moment it has been looking for, the moment it sought me for.

I feel more settled now, accepting my fate. Right, so be it you bastard, let us see how skilled you are. You expected an easy kill, you almost had me, but you have made a mistake tonight, I am made of sterner stuff than you realise. You came here for violence and death, but even those who are the prey sometimes fight back, fight back with such venom filled fury, that the hunter becomes the hunted. Prepare to die!

Anger, raw animal anger, courses through my veins and I leap from the sofa, leaving the warmth of my long forgotten peace and slumber. My muscles are primed and strong, my teeth are sharp, my claws sharper; you who bring death, prepare to meet your maker, prepare to meet your demise! Our eyes meet, they are wide and surprised, I feel reassured, it hadn't expected its quarry to attack and be more aggressive than it could ever be. I fly through the air, the tension has been released, I am not just ready for this, I was born for this and have been waiting for my moment, the demon is a fool, I am in fight mode now. The room can't contain me as I race across the wooden floor, slipping slightly as I rush towards *it*, the beast who came to kill me. Its limbs raise, its claws extend and I can see it is ready to strike, but so am I.

I skid to a halt, realising the windows and door are shut tight. We glare at each other, if only there was a way to get to you, I would rip you from limb to limb, it would be a fight of the titans, a fight to the death. I would taste *your* fear and drink *your* blood. I would, if only I could get to you.

The beast raises its head towards the light, it obviously thinks it still has a chance. A muscular black and menacing paw is put on the glass with sharp claws proud and taps the window.

Tap, tap, tap.

The screeching noise commences again as its claws move down the window. A slight smile transforms the would be killers face as it moves from the last of the shadows fully into the light, from a beast to... Wilma.

"WIILMAAAAA! You cow! I'll kill you, I'll rip you from limb to limb! Wait until I get my paws on you, you should know better than to come here, you've made a biiiig mistake and will pay. I'll..."

From the next room comes banging and an angry deep voice shouts "Oi! Oi! Bloody hell, stop that sodding racket and stop meowing!"

How dare they shout at me, it is their fault I am locked in here unable to defend my territory, our haven. They will pay as well, after they have fed me in the morning anyways.

My attention returns to the window. "Wilma, just you wait!" I hiss. How dare she wake me. We stare at each other, I now realise she did this on purpose, invading my privacy in the dark of the night, knowing I am locked in here every night, just to scare me. I have been stupid, my stupid imagination has got carried away and I feel silly, I was safe, there was no monster, just the bloody cat from next door. Not just any cat though, Wilma - my nemesis!

Wilma looks at me with victory filled eyes, she knows she had me, that she scared me good and proper, albeit momentarily. She got what she wanted and is pleased with herself. I won't get back to sleep now, but you wait Wilma, your time will come. Indeed it will come!

With one last menacing, but ever so slightly gleeful stare, Wilma turns her back, walks over to the plant pot on our terrace, hops in and relieves herself. The final indignity, that will smell in the sunshine tomorrow and I will probably be blamed, again! Finished, she wanders over towards the window again for one final gloat, then haughtily turns her back on me and heads off down the steps.

It takes a while for my breathing to calm down as I am still pumped up with fear, anger and embarrassment. Finally, all is quiet and I know she won't return, my heart rate slows and the night once again gets back to normal. Oh well, I hope my spot on the sofa is still warm, perhaps I will have time for a little nap after all. Maybe I will be able to lose myself in my favourite little dream space again and forget the night's excitement. I soon return to my slumbers, but spend my time dreaming of what I will do to bloody Wilma in the morning.

Whale Watching

T he door crashes opens and in it comes, dragging its feet across the floor, acting like a drugged sloth, making an intolerable scratching noise with no respect for me, my need for sleep, nor my privacy. You would think he bloody well owns the place, strolling past, talking about a "Good morning" or something and blathering on as if I give a shit. Bloody fool even ruffles my fur, every which way, and bends down so I can look at his ugly mug and smell his foul, rank breath that smells spicy and fetid, what an animal.

"One more stroke and your history buddy, the paws of power will strike and you'll be a goner, you've no idea how close you're treading to a world of pain. Don't mess with my bloody fur, especially after the night I've had!" I hiss at him.

"Aww, happy to see me are ya," he says, looking pleased as though he is the funniest clown in town. "You were a noisy puddy cat last night weren't you, eh? Being brave and defending us from the other mean cats again were ya? Haha."

I give him my hardest, most menacing stare; yes, very funny. He has no idea what I have to put up with. Why I share this building with them is beyond me, lots of people would do a much better job I am sure and be better company as well as being a bit more respectful and kind too. Who wants to be woken up this early after the night I just had? Having run out of things to say, and he is definitely a few biscuits short of a breakfast this one, he shuffles off to the tap, fills up the kettle and turns it on so it can add to the unbearable noise with its dull roar that gets ever louder until steam comes out the top and starts to twirl around under the cupboard. Seemingly satisfied at the disturbance he has caused, he gets the plastic container out of the cupboard, staggers like the moron he is over to my food bowl, pours in a few meagre, barely edible biscuits in to the *dirty* bowl before muttering "there you go my brave soldier." For some reason that only he knows, he then proceeds to open the back door as wide as it goes, just to let some cold air and noise in. I am sure he only does this to annoy me, before shuffling off to make two cups of steaming something and then heading back out; I bet his room is warmer.

Once he has gone, my mood improves as things are slightly better and at least the room is in peace once again, although the fool has woken me up good and proper now and made the room unbearably chilly in the process too. Thanks. Oh how very droll and thoughtful he is, I feel honoured. Honoured that he made such an effort to wake me up so nicely and prepare my delicious food so lovingly. Honoured that he put so much thought into giving me the same old unimaginative cardboard snacks he throws into the bowl every morning with the usual mix of half falling in the bowl and the other half on the floor for me to eat. Honestly, I am not an animal you know. Oh yes, he is a keeper isn't he? Reluctantly, I hop down from my warm spot on the sofa and walk over to the bowl where, even though the sight and smell disgust me, I tuck in. I can't help myself, after all, I have been caged up like an animal and left to starve all night and needs must.

Ooh, yum, I do like these, my favourite!

Having eaten my fill of the nauseating food that had been carelessly thrown everywhere for me to eat like a stupid and starving dog, I need to quench my thirst to get rid of the taste. Drinking warm water from the rather unclean bowl with hairs floating in it simply reminds me that the people that share my living space are tediously and predictably unhygienic and uncouth. Finished, I decide to head outside, it is a good job I made the tiresome creature thing open the door; they may take my dignity, but they will never take my freedom.

The first thing that strikes me is the smell, there is an awful odour in the air this morning, the smell is pungent and clings to the back of my throat. I can almost taste something rather unpleasant in my mouth, although I must admit to it being familiar. My mind must still be half asleep as I can't think straight after last night's excitement. Hang on, I know what the smell is... I turn my head and see the earth scattered below the plant pot on the terrace and it all comes back. Reluctantly I find myself being unconsciously dragged to the pot to witness the crime. I gag. That is really disgusting, she needs to eat healthy biscuits rather than decaying animal in jelly as it is obviously not a healthy diet for her. Wow, the people she shares her place with must really hate her. The thought pleases me, then I think that as the crime has already been committed, I may as well make the most of the situation and get some benefit from it as Wilma will get the blame.

No sooner have I finished, than I hear a banging on the window and see the female sloth thing shouting and waving her arms at me. Typical, bloody typical. It is so unfair, I get the blame for everything! It reminds me, I must make Wilma pay.

"Hey, sod you! I wasn't here first you know, it was bloody Wilma," I shout at them, "you should give her a right smack, she's a dirty cow who really needs to improve her diet."

"We must have the only cat that tries to look cute by meowing while crapping in a plant pot with an audience," female sloth thing says, laughing at her so called humour to the pig next to her. I give up, there is no hope for those two.

"Yeah, that's one strange but cute cat all right," he says, looking at me while I sit there feeling rather embarrassed. I quickly finish off and clean up as best I can, under the rather undignified circumstances, and wait for my moment.

"Anyway, I'd better be off or I'll never catch the tube. Loves ya," he shouts. With that he tries to rush out of the door, but this is the moment I have been waiting for, he is at his most vulnerable now, in a rush while dressed in his dark suit and he has to get past me. It is the perfect storm. He is too tempting a target, so I rush over, playing the affectionate cutie he so wants me to be, and rub my way all round his legs before he has a chance to react. "Ha!" I squeal with delight. All the time he is dancing like a ballerina trying to avoid me, but he has no chance, I am an expert at this. Before he is able to move, his lower legs are covered in my hair and I feel rather smug with myself. It may be seen by others as a rather myopic victory, but it pleases me no end, I got him, again! It is our daily routine and he never learns. A look of horror crosses his face and then I can see the troubled look that gives me so much pleasure. He has a choice now, miss the tube or go to work covered in me. He decides quicker than normal today, so he must be in a rush, perfect! He half heartedly brushes his legs off with his hands as best he can, while hoping from leg to leg try and keep me away from doing even more damage, before racing off down the stairs muttering to himself. Mission accomplished!

The female sloth just shakes her head and heads back into the bedroom.

Feeling pretty bloody pleased with myself, I decide it is time to find a sunny sheltered patch so I can try and warm up a bit and show myself to the world in the process. After all, my world loves me.

Outside has been magically transformed from the previously silent, dark and sinister place of the night before, that was full of dangerous beasts and demons, in to a bright but chilly, bustling and noisy city landscape. Rush hour in the city. Cars and buses crawling along the busy road, horns lazily blaring out every now and then, adult occupants catching quick glimpses of their phones in between braking and slowing to a stop. Children chatting, laughing, playing and pressing their faces to the steamy breath covered windows in the back of the almost stationary vehicles while watching the world go by, always on the look out for some exciting event to catch their sleepy little eyes and hook their fertile imaginations. Buses are crammed full of people, like cattle being taken to slaughter, uncomfortable, morose, silent. Surely, no one would willingly choose to be there, day after day, going through the daily indignity of squeezing into a red tube, to be squashed like sardines in a slow moving warm musky tin, desperately trying to secure whatever space and privacy they can by gently easing out a small space for themselves and then hiding in a newspaper or, more usually, a phone, but they seem to nonetheless. There, but never quite present, blocking the close confining proximity of humanity from their conscious thoughts as best they can with the invisible barriers that they build around themselves — never wanting to break the seeming unspoken rule of ignoring everyone else, but still being conscious enough to try and make room for others, obviously never acknowledging their presence, whilst huffing and feeling angry at having to further shrink their virtual privacy screens and walls of protection. Commuting etiquette in action. Life isn't visible in this claustrophobic press of humanity, it is hidden away in their minds that are dreaming of either better times to come or those that have already been. During the rush hour, life is virtual and in the cloud and physically separate from reality, people are with their far away friends, looking at the happy smiling faces of the few they do know rather than acknowledging those present that they don't. Always trying to be somewhere else to escape the horror of the here and now, to momentarily avoid the reality of having to go to work, but always preparing for the jostling rushed exit from the bus, ready to walk the final stages to work and then hide away in a myriad of jobs. Whilst a lucky few love their daily work life, for the vast majority it is just a chore, another chore in an already difficult life; no wonder they try and escape.

    Pavements are full of commuters all marching silently to the destiny of their days-to-be, heads down, hands in pockets, withdrawn into their own individual worlds. Smartly dressed sombre business suits with £500 shoes sharply contrast with the more relaxed and ubiquitous attire of jeans, trainers, hoodies and coats in every colour that could make a gloriously colourful painting of the tapestry of life, if only anyone paid attention and ignored the somber and stony faces. Everyone is different, yet everyone is the same; a horde of wildebeest on some sort of automatic migration rushing through their lives and accepting their destinations without conscious thought. Every now and then some laughter lifts above the background noise of engines revving, horns blaring and some light chatter, but most is only ever from single commuters, looking ahead, seeing their path, but not really observing life as they chat into their phones to far away friends. Always somewhere else, never really present, smiling at those who aren't here and scowling at those who are. Some look determined, the ones with purpose, they move with resolve and pace, weaving their way through the slower moving people who move like flotsam on a calm sea, just drifting slowly with the current. Headphones are jammed into ears bombarded with blaring music that no-one else can hear, personal and connected direct in to their inner minds, shutting everything else out.

Bikes weave between traffic and along the edges of the road. Racing bikes with riders clad in lycra, helmeted, serious, focused, angry at being held up; no red lights or cars will stop them. Others move slowly, just content to be moving slightly faster than under their own power, some even enjoy it, but not many, most are on auto-pilot.

The morning commute in all its magnificent obscurity; life dictates the pace, what choices do they really have — commute, work, commute, eat, sleep, repeat. Present, but never really truly here, everyone together yet completely isolated, thinking about the past, dreaming about the future, worrying and planning. Always worrying and planning.

Cat perches on its spot in the sun, trying to soak up the first of the ever so slightly warming rays that promise a lovely spring day ahead. Stretching and just watching the passing tide of humanity, all extras in Cat's play of life, watching people who are as unimportant to it as they are to each other, we are all the Stars of our own show and why should the Star ever take an interest in the extras?

Wow, they are like ants, every day is the same. Where do they all come from and where do they go? Look at them, crawling along the road in their unimportant lives, seemingly oblivious to where they are going, being drawn somewhere against their wishes, moths to a flame, haha.

Come on fatty, keep on moving, that's it, try and keep up. And you chubster.

Hey old man, shuffling well today and all dressed up, funeral is it? It'll be yours soon enough don't you worry, look at you, you must be at least three hundred years old, why hang around, what are you waiting for, certainly not excitement? I hope you don't die just yet though, wait until you are round the corner, I hate those sirens and that would be another bloody inconvenience.

That's it, chop chop, better beat the others eh, haha, in a rush because you were too lazy to get up on time are you, you lazy twat? Wow, you is u.g.l.y, you ain't got no alibi. Where on earth do these people come from, Uglyville? I hate this time of day, it is busy and clogged with fumes that stick in the back of my throat, it stinks, it is noisy, there are so many ugly people and I can't get to the park. May as well nip inside for a quick snooze while you lot sort yourselves out, go on, sod right off and leave me in peace.

Back inside, things are quieter. The noise outside will continue for a while yet and there is little chance of me being able to get over to the park, so I am trapped in this flea pit once more. Everything seems hectic and busy, yet everyone moves so slowly, there are so many people, all angry and alone, on their way to somewhere of no real importance. Then it will be the turn of all the children, the young ones with their parents and the older ones in groups, going to school. Life seems so much happier then, albeit still bloody annoying, with everyone laughing and joking, but at least the youngsters seem to be alive, something about growing up must mean people have all the fun sucked out of them for some reason. Then it goes quiet with just the old, the slow, the lazy and the dog owners about. It is always the same routine, there is no real need to rush and so I just need to bide my time and wait for it all to settle down.

Perched on the top of the kitchen cupboard, I can keep an eye on the comings and goings outside whilst feeling secure enough to relax. What to do? Eat, sleep, or… well, there isn't really much else for it until later I guess, so I may as well do both!

Female sloth comes into the room with her phone and headphones in hand. Dressed in her well worn 'comfies', or tatty scruffs as they could otherwise be called, she pulls a large cushion from the sofa, places it on the floor and lowers herself onto it before crossing her legs, straightening her back, touching the phone, placing it in front of her and finally putting the headphones on. Eyes closed, she sits there, still and silent, just breathing and looking content, not saying a word, opening her eyes or moving.

After a couple of minutes, I am drawn to the solitary and still figure, drawn towards the calming presence on the cushion, looking so at peace while the world outside rushes by. Despite knowing this is a private moment I don't stop, I can't stop, this is outside of my control. I am drawn towards the female sloth and start walking round and round her body, rubbing against her knees, back and sides as I go. Round and round, rubbing against the figure that remains upright, silent, unmoving and seemingly unaware of my presence. I don't want to, but cannot help myself, I can feel the relaxation and calmness emanating from the cross legged figure on the floor, and enjoy the sensation of rubbing my way round and round and slowly round…

Suddenly I stop, I am almost on her lap now and just watch the female sloth. I know I have intruded on a special moment, but it felt right and I couldn't help myself, the closeness made me feel relaxed and calm too. Also, I know it will probably bug the shit out of the female while she was meditating, even though I know she wouldn't react in any away, it still felt good to know that I must have slightly irritated her though. She always likes to pretend she doesn't sense me here, but everyday I know she does, it is our little secret.

Finally the female finishes. Taking her headphones off, she stands up, gives me one of *those* looks, then picks me up, rubs my fur, dumps me on the terrace and shuts the door. I won the battle, sloth won the war; same routine, every day.

With a last look at the retreating form inside, I set off to check what is going on in the world, defend my territory and travel the known world once more. I get to the wall at the bottom of the stairs, before climbing up to have a rest and watch the last of the commuters and children flood by.

Come on, keep it moving, baaa! Wow, you are one ugly chubby kid sunshine, bet your parents are proud. Come on mum, make the effort and at least get out of your Pjs before taking dumb little princess to school. Ha, you're destined to fail and be miserable curly, so are you shorty, and you, jeez you're a tall arse aren't ya.

With the morning encouragements done for another day, it is time for a cheeky nap somewhere secluded while this lot sods off methinks.

Walking the Hood

The morning rush soon finishes and life returns to a semblance of peace and normality, well, as peaceful and normal as you can get in the city. There is always some weirdo out and about, either rushing around late for an appointment, or ambling aimlessly along to meet friends. Traffic flows more freely, people have a bit more space and can breathe and move, tempers calm and life picks up a beat and seems just that little bit happier. The ever present dull roar of airplanes hangs in the background, overhead and in the distance, trails of cotton wool vapour firming into solid white arrows with the metal tips holding the lucky few who are going somewhere, anywhere; anyone on the ground who looks up casts ever so slightly envious glances whenever they come into consciousness. Every now and then the screeching shrill of sirens can be heard on the breeze, sometimes close, sometimes not, but always cutting through the calm and announcing an emergency and suffering for some unfortunate soul who hadn't expected their day to turn out this way.

Cat is woken from its mid-mid-morning nap by the smell of sweet cherry wafting across the path in thick fuggy clouds that seem so heavy they just hang in the breeze with a seeming permanence one moment, before evaporating and dispersing the next, leaving no trace of their brief existence. The smell is delicious, perhaps a bit too sweet, but so much better than the choking foul stench of burning tobacco that all too often offends

Cat's nostrils, that is horrible. The next puff hangs and lingers on the air and is followed by a squeal of laughter; noise, always noise. No chance of sleeping here, best get on with the patrol. With a sudden burst of energy, which is unusual for this time of the day, Cat has a good stretch and jumps down to look at the cause of the disturbance.

The youngish looking lady with her long brown hair is sat on the doorstep of her flat in the sun, which seems to be her favourite spot in the mornings, vaping and playing with her irritating and slightly weird son. Always bloody laughing those two, well, when she's not just sat there vacantly staring across the road daydreaming. What have they got to be so happy about? They live with Wilma for goodness' sake, must be awful, but they are probably all as bad as each other, what a disgusting bunch, they deserve each other. Why do they have to live near me anyway? And what have they got to be happy about, nothing as far as I can see. They never seem to do anything, yet they are always making a bloody noise. Nice cherry vape smell though.

Deciding the time is right, I set off, hugging the side of the low wall for protection. At the entrance to the flats a few houses down, next to a big terracotta plant pot, I stop. I always makes this slight detour, just because I can, no real reason really, but why should there be? I sniff the air and can smell *it*, I always can, it is disgusting, I can smell Wilma and can tell she was here very recently. She really should have more respect for where she lives. I look up and see the young lady is looking directly at me again, she always seems to follow my progress for some reason I can't figure out. It is creepy if you ask me. I turn my back on her as haughtily as I can and feign disinterest, after all, I am too good for this place, far too good. Looking up and down the street I can see there is a suitable pause in the tide of humanity. It looks safe and so, with a final check, I dash across the road, under the black metal fence with the sharp menacing spikes on top of each stake, and enter the park.

The park. My park. My world.

A deep breath and a quick scan of the area to make sure there isn't any danger lurking in the bushes; all seems quiet. My senses are always on high alert at this time, the pavement and road are dangerous places and I have seen, all too often, what can happen to the unwary; it is not pleasant. One morning there was a fox cub by the side of the road, or what was left of the cub. It must have been hit by a truck, squashed, its life extinguished when it was least expected, a journey unfinished, a task left undone, a life unfulfilled. All very unpleasant and everyone felt slightly nauseous when they saw it the first day, but soon lost interest as it decomposed and slowly disappeared, becoming just an inconvenient eyesore to the living passing by in their important lives. I know I have to be careful, but also know that as long as I am, I am invincible. I am strong, powerful, clever, and better than the others, better than all the inconsequential and unimportant masses. Danger means nothing to me, well, apart from when it is dark, or there are loud noises, or people, or cars, or buses, or dogs, cats or even large birds, especially crows. Apart from that, I am unstoppable!

The mid mid-morning park is a bit of a hit and miss affair, Cat knows the open space, which is interspersed with islands of trees, bushes and plants, several meandering paths crossing every which way and a few street lights, could contain anything at this time of day; not quite as bad as after dark, but not entirely safe either. Children skipping school, smoking, causing mischief, shouting, giggling in their conspiracies and schemes, throwing stones at cats for fun. Parents with wild pre-school kids running amok, squealing with pleasure in their own little worlds of wonder, racing and chasing anything within their sights, including cats. Then there were the drunks and homeless, securing any privacy that they can, hiding from the weather, people and life. They are never any real problem, they don't chase or laugh, they just stare, stare and mumble incomprehensibly; they look scary though and so Cat never trusts them, never goes close, who knows what they might do? Dog walkers are the worst though, not the people themselves, although they are bad enough as you can never trust a person who likes dogs, but rather the dogs themselves. Running, always bloody running, after anything and everything. Many a time Cat has had to dive into a thorny bush to escape their evil clutches; they are just lucky Cat doesn't stand its ground and rip them apart, oh how Cat has been tempted, but for the goodness of its heart, they would be in trouble! Then there is the fact that the boy dogs can't walk past a tree, lamppost or bush without cocking their legs. Man that stinks, it is so uncouth. The only thing that does make Cat smile, is watching the owners picking up the dogs' poo and then swinging it around in a little bag as they carry on walking; how on earth the dogs have trained them so well is beyond Cat, but it is a trick it would like to learn. Then there are the other cats, how dare they come into Cat's world! Many a time such chance encounters has resulted in a clash of claws; never has Cat been beaten, well apart from a few unlucky times, but they aren't worth dwelling on. No, this is Cat's sanctuary and Cat has rights!

The only good thing about this time of day is that there is no chance of meeting Wilma. For some unknown and bizarre reason, she prefers the night, presumably to hide her hideousness and to socialise with the other demons that lurk in the darkness, and because she is deranged of course. The thought reminds Cat that perhaps it ought to return last night's favour and find one of Wilma'a plant pots.

The park is quiet, all clear, and the morning patrol can proceed. Moving through the open landscape is heavenly, space to breathe and roam freely. The Eastern side of the park is more densely vegetated and covered in trees, ideal stalking territory, as long as you don't stray into the play park and keep away from the big concrete bowl where the older kids hang around skateboarding. Keeping to the trees, bypassing the danger zones, Cat continues at a leisurely pace, constantly vigilant, looking, hunting. This is Cat's Serengeti and it grows in size, ferocity and power with each stride, looking for prey and victims to torment. Well, one wouldn't want to actually catch anything, claws get mucky, paws dirty and you might get hurt. Not through inability, oh no, Cat is a killer, just a very restrained killer; in fact, Cat actually thinks itself above such base behaviour, but it is still king of the beasts, well king of the park, well…

The birds respect the beast and scatter at Cat's approach, apart from a brave Robin who stands its ground, looking defiant until the last second and then flying to the nearest branch; it must have known Cat is just taking it easy today, else it would have been very sorry. A few squirrels cling to the side of trees, defying gravity, running around the bark and then hopping to the ground and racing along like fluffy stones skimming over a flat pond, all the while looking annoyingly cute; what the purpose of them is, Cat has no idea. More things just to make up the numbers, more prey in the Serengeti, put there in its world just in case it does ever decided to hunt.

Towards the border, guarded by another spiked metal fence to keep the prey in and the unwanted out, runs another road, quieter than Cat's, but busy enough to be wary of, with a huge dark red brick building running along its entire length. The area around the block of flats is quieter than the front of the park, that is just bedlam. Here, there are still people coming and going, and cars and bikes on the road, but far fewer at this time of day. Cat decides to relax in some long grass by the fence, after all, it has been patrolling for some time and needs to retain strength, just in case. Gazing lazily at the flats, Cat observes the dark inhospitable building, the bleakness of the bricks broken by a myriad of colourful curtains in every window, some closed, more pulled open. Dull net curtains crumpled and askew, allowing some form of privacy against those who would look in, but greying out the colour of life for those looking out. Bikes stand awkwardly on one wheel upright on balconies, children's toys, clothes hanging from sagging lines, mattresses stuffed into small balconies, all seemingly forgotten. Some balconies have borders of flowers and plants in little pots, colour and life contrasting with the harshness of the dark lifeless bricks. Laughter and the noise from radios and televisions that are never switched off hang in the air; life, of sorts. All is lost on Cat, it is just the border, the end of its known world, the end of its interest, nothing really matters past the fence.

I decide to be brave as I like to push myself every now and again and live on the edge, so on the spur of the moment I do something out of the ordinary, I nip out from the safety of the grass, under the fence and sit on the cold path. Outside of my domain, conquering new lands, I sit and look around, feeling proud and safe. The relative quietness is broken by a haggard looking lady, wearing a pristine white apron over old worn jeans, ungainly pushing and bouncing an old bike, down the stairs; clunk, clunk, clunk, clunk, ting! I almost have a heart attack at the unexpected noise, hackles are raised, but I decide the old lady seems harmless enough, so I continue watching. The bike is rolled all the way down the hard concrete stairs with little thought as the lady seems uncaring and barely functioning. At the bottom, she leans the bike against the wall and nips back up the stairs before coming back down with an old carrier bag she trows in the tatty wicker basket on the handlebars. As she is putting on her helmet, she stares at me and I am momentarily shocked to be noticed, so just stare back, holding her gaze as I want her to look away first. Suddenly, I almost poop myself as a noisy motorbike revs at the top of the road and the harsh deep throaty roar nosily reverberates off the flats and all down the road. This is way too much for me, so I quickly nip back under the fence and back into the wilderness and my sanctuary.

Calmed, focused and determined, Cat continues on its morning patrol and the lady is soon forgotten; after all, why would Cat want to remember anyone so insignificant? The bushes and trees now shield it from the worst of humanity, the noise is softened and the presence of people hidden. Despite being littered with ever present rubbish, Cat likes this spot as few people ever come in to this part and so it is safe. Moving deeper into the expanse, Cat stops. It is near the main path that runs through the park, there are people walking along, using the park as a shortcut rather than a place of conscious tranquility, either chatting on phones or just walking with their heads down, moving with quick purpose, simply focussed on their next destination. Just off the path a woman dressed in black is running, a small white dog on a lead running by her side and then bursting off and pulling her along, enjoying the exercise and being outside. Further out there is another person throwing a ball far into the distance, a big black and white collie racing off to retrieve it and take it back to the owner, continuously repeating the sequence; neither dog nor owner getting bored.

What a complete waste of time, bloody simpletons. At least they are all occupied and will leave me alone, best for them, else I would ruin their day Cat says to itself. Of course, it knows it shouldn't be speaking to itself, it needs to be silent and stealthy, it just can't help itself sometimes.

Cat moves down and through the bushes parallel to the path, it needs to find the safest place to cross, somewhere where there is cover on both sides. It freezes just before the perfect spot, hearing the dreaded sounds of laughter and conspiratorial chatter, then silence, then raised voices, more cackling laughter and finally more silence. Continuing to listen, Cat moves slowly, stealthily, towards the edge of the bush, near the top of this side of the park by the corner gate. A group of teenagers, a couple of boys and three girls, sit on the low wall, in school uniforms that don't hide the fact that they are neither at school nor very uniform. Bare legs for the girls, skirts that shouldn't cost very much if priced on the amount of fabric they use, baggy trousers for the boys, shirts hanging out, dark blue sweatshirts and ties worn long and thin, short and fat, knotted rather than tied, around their necks. Smoking, looking at phones, and laughing, enjoying the camaraderie of skipping school together, the feeling of control, controlling their destinies, of freedom. Freedom, but not from their phones — the perpetual glow illuminates their faces under the shadows of the trees, all are absorbed in their own phone, laughing at their owns worlds, connected, but not to each other. Together, yet alone, but happy enough.

Bloody kids, it is just my luck they have chosen to loiter here of all places. I need to cross the path, so I have to waste my valuable time hiding here, watching and waiting for the right moment to run unnoticed across the harsh coldness of the path to the safety of the bushes on the far side. I look up and am startled, for the second time this morning, to discover that I am being watched, again! The girl on the end is watching, or rather staring at me intently, with her phone raised and pointing directly towards me. Rarely does anyone have the skill to see me, I am usually a master of concealment and only seen by prey just before I pounce, when it is too late for them to avoid me. Well, that would be the case if ever I decided to anyway. This girl, however, the one with the long steel grey coloured hair, a colour that she will naturally become in later life but then deliberately turn back to the colour of her youth, has me firmly in her sights. I must be under the weather today, I can't understand how I have lost my touch all of a sudden. Unsettled, I am momentarily uncertain what to do and so simply stare back in shock. It is a mistake as I should never remain still once seen. A boy next to the girl looks up, casually casts his cigarette to one side, looks at the steel haired girl, follows her gaze, also sees me, and then launches a drinks can on the path right in front of me. I explode into action, leaving the clattering metallic noise mixed with laughter behind, and rush across the track, running further and further into the bushes the other side, escaping from the harm and hurt of people. Bastards.

The Southern border is the part Cat generally likes least, the open grassland makes it feel vulnerable, but on the plus side there is little chance of ambush. Well, apart from kids throwing stones, bikes and dogs of course. This section is always taken at speed, fast and focused; clearly never too much speed, Cat does have to maintain control and look graceful after all, and it would have to stop half way for a quick breather if it overdid it, and that would be disastrous and rather unseemly.

Arriving at the Western edge of its known world, Cat is much happier as this part is full of flower beds, a tennis court, scrubland, bushes and trees. Very pleasant. Finding a spot in a luxuriously soft flower bed right next to the fence, Cat looks out into the world beyond. Another road, but wide and quiet. Big houses, posh cars, new 4x4s, tended and manicured gardens at the front; no net curtains here, just the odd slatted blind with clean and clear windows that almost invite those outside to look in to see the wealth, see the possessions. Clinical, precise, expensive, but ultimately lifeless. It is quiet, no televisions or radios blaring, but no laughter either. If the outside fences of the park were the teeth of a giant zip that was slowly fastened shut, hiding the park and pulling the two sides slowly together, moving the flats and the houses towards each other, the contrast would be blindingly clear for all to see, and horrific. The haves and the have-nots, the rich and the poor, the employees and the employers. Luckily for all though, there is no zip, the shield provided by the park is a permanent fixture that prevents any uncomfortable comparisons, so no one will see ever the sharp contrast as it really is, it will remain hidden to most, just different sides of the park; acceptable, and just so. Cat sees nothing, no contrast, no wealth, just another spot, another border, its only suspicion is that the biscuits would probably be a bit tastier if it chose to live here.

A door slams and makes me cautiously look around. I can see a man as he leaves one of the houses across the road that looks large enough to house several large families, with room to spare. The man scowls at his phone as soon as the door is shut and is totally absorbed. I watch him walk along the road, totally focused on the small device in his hand, only looking up momentarily to maintain footing, walking at pace next to the fence in his dark expensive suit, crisp white shirt and ever so shiny brogues. He looks a right looser to me, but probably a well to do expensive looser no doubt. As soon as he nears, an overpowering scent with a ghastly chemical sharp smell attacks my senses. It almost makes me gag and my eyes water it is that strong, it is bloody awful. Why on earth would anyone want to put that muck on themselves, it can't be good for them. It is so overpoweringly strong and horrendous smelling that I can't maintain my natural statue-like stance and sneeze, repeatedly. I have really lost my skills today and need to get home and have a lie down! The man looks up from his phone and, for the first time since leaving his house, a smile creases his face as he looks at me whilst I am involuntarily sneezing and just wallowing in the flower beds. Bastard!

Rarely does Cat sneeze, it is not what skilled predators do. Clearly the man had an anti-ambush musk that affects trained killers; Cat decides it must watch out for that in future, it can't have anything affecting its abilities, it is embarrassing. Rubbing its nose, Cat reluctantly decides that is enough of the nice side of the park and it is time to get some fresh air and complete the loop.

Cat heads back towards the noisier end of the park, back towards home and that nice comfy sofa. Another expedition completed and the world is safe, so Cat can relax, job done. Well, a good predator never truly lets its guard down, so Cat keeps vigilant, only thinking about some milk, mackerel, biscuits and a nap fleetingly. Back at the boundary, Cat quickly dashes under the fence, has a quick check for traffic and runs then over the road in a flash.

Slightly out of breath, Cat pauses on the pavement at the far side of the road from the park, next to the small house just along the road from its flat. A favourite spot, there is a small garden here that provides a bit of sanctuary, a little island of tranquillity in the chaotic city if ever Cat is nearly caught out in this exposed spot. The garden is always worth a quick peruse, often there is a little bowl of tuna chunks, even though it doesn't smell as if a cat lives there, which is odd. Even stranger is that the tuna is always fresh, not decaying and rotting like lots of food left in bowls, that wouldn't do, Cat is not an animal after all.

A quick scan of the area and a sniff declares it is safe. The bowl is there and I feel like I deserve a quick snack, after all, I have just spent ages in the wilderness keeping the known world safe from predators, which is all really rather hungry work. As tasty as the treat is, I can't help but be slightly annoyed that there isn't anything left out for me to drink, so I am forced to go and drink the rather delicious water in the old metal watering can; needs must.

Suddenly, I sense I am being watched and know it is the old

stupid git who lives here, watching through the window, lazy old weird sod. He is always there, creepily watching, looking old and useless as he stands by the window in his pyjamas whilst slowly decaying as old people do — you can always smell the decay on them. Disgusted, I turn my back and disdainfully walk out of the garden, down the last stretch of road, up the stairs and back home.

More of a hovel than a home really, Cat really ought to think about moving, it is a wild animal, not a pet and shouldn't be constrained and cooped up like a stupid dog or person; it needs its freedom. Perhaps it will consider that tomorrow, the sofa looks quite inviting and it might as well have a little nap, after a few biscuits. Got to keep in tip top condition.

Clare - Hard Work, Hurt & Heartache

"Goooooooood morning you lovely people, it's six o'clock, so rise and shine my lovelies! It's a super lovely day out here today and you don't want to miss a second of it because I know you're going to be fabulous. Thanks for listening to the Logan Coss Breakfast Show here on City Two FM and boy oh boy have I got some great things for you coming up in today's show. More of that later though as first I need to make sure you're wide awake and ready to go! Soooooo, let's start things off with the amazing…"

"Oh my days, enough of that shite," I hear someone say, then I realise it is me, half asleep, in the groggy murky world between wakefulness and sleep. I can't take the false happiness for too long else I might well vomit, I need to wake up first, it is just a slightly better way to be woken up than one of the many annoying tunes on my phone. I hit the top of the radio alarm clock to shut Logan Coss up for a few minutes and give me a moment's respite. No one can really be that happy this time of the day; no one, ever.

Not quite believing it is really six o'clock already, I struggle to get motivated; shite.

I lie here for a few minutes, trying to will myself to tumble out of bed, stumble to the kitchen and pour myself a much needed cup of ambition. But as I don't have a career, or future prospects of any sort, a simple cup of coffee will do. With enormous reluctance, I push the duvet off, swing my leaden legs over the side and stand up before my mind can protest and prevent me from doing what I must. Up, albeit wobbly, I have a yawn and a stretch and try to come to life before heading for the kitchen; dirty plates, a bowl and glasses greet me that will all need to be cleared away before I can finally enjoy my morning fix of caffeine. Shit, there is always a payback, it seemed such a good idea to leave everything when I was too tired to clear up last night, now it is just another task to make an otherwise crap day slightly crappier from the outset. I am briefly tempted just to leave them, make my coffee and pretend I didn't see them, that is what my daughter would do, and hope a fairy godmother sorts it all out for me while I am at work. No, I know there are no short cuts in life, no fairy godmothers and no-one to help; you can't run from what needs to be done, problems just remain, and get worse if ignored, so if you do the crime, pay the time. I just need to get on with it as I will be too knackered again later and need to keep everything just about manageable. If only I could hide the dishes, hide from life, just for a few days.

 Dishes washed, kitchen cleaned, I grab my coffee and take a long satisfying sip, filling my mouth with the hot liquid that is so full of the much needed rocket fuel demanded so badly by my body to help me to really get going. Enjoying the coffee, I put the radio back on and Logan 'so-frikin-happy-and-funny' Coss introduces another annoyingly chirpy ear worm that will get everyone motivated and stick in their heads for the rest of the day; this one isn't too bad and I am sure I've heard Beau playing it. In fact, it is a surprisingly good and catchy tune, I get completely absorbed in the song as I cross my legs and start humming the tune as I listen to the words, something about being caught in a bad romance, it makes me chuckle as it could have been written for me. Before long my suspended foot is bouncing away in time with the beat seemingly of its own accord. Catching myself humming and tapping along makes me think of Beau, she cringes and gets so embarrassed if ever I do this when we are out or she has friends round. I smile as I think about her, my little girl, now 16 and strongly independent, able to feel embarrassment in *me* and who I am; it seems like only yesterday when she was a helpless bundle of devoted fun and I was her world. Time flies and I have no idea where it goes, just that it does and it often does so creating memories of hard work, hurt and heartache rather than happiness and relaxation along the way. The good memories are there somewhere, they just need to be given time to rediscover them. Time, it is always about time…

With a jolt, I realise I am running late. I shouldn't waste precious time day dreaming, life just moves on and there is too much to do, the endless cycle can never be controlled and we just need to keep focused else we will be left even further behind. Even Logan Coss seems to have lost his edge and run out of steam; perhaps he gulps down a sugary coffee at 5:59am and then just goes on a quick fire burst of high octane happiness fuelled by his sugary caffeine high. The additional energy never lasts long and then life catches up and the struggles begin; life is not easy, but no-one ever said it would be. Well done Logan, 20 minutes in and nearly two hours to go, but you have already peaked; never peak too early Mr Coss. Shit, I need to get going, no time to relax, the bills won't pay themselves and I have an early appointment to get to in Liverpool Street. The teenage illusion that life is full of eat, sleep, rave, repeat comes to mind — if only it were true and life was one long party. Work, eat, sleep, repeat sneaks up on you before you know it and becomes the norm. Work always comes first and life just wears you down somehow.

Hopping in the shower, I enjoy the sensation of hot water flowing over me, caressing me, cleansing the body I was once so naively proud of and others adored. That was so long ago now, when I actually had a life of dreams before me and I had the luxury of never having to face reality and think about things too much. Life comes easy to the young, but seems a struggle at the time; if only they knew, if only Beau knew what would happen to her when she is older. Perhaps it is best they don't know and the isolation, naivety and selfishness are just natural in-built defence mechanisms to ensure we don't give up on life too soon. Thanks Mother Nature, thanks for lulling us into a false sense of security with our pert tits, tight flawless skin, energy, few worries and hope before crushing us when we get older and actually have the freedoms we so desperately desired. Just as we get going, life cruelly strangles all hope from us before we even have a chance to realise what is happening. Poor Beau.

Wishing I had time for a longer shower, or indeed the money to pay for it, I have hopped out of the shower and in to the coldness of the bathroom to dry myself, all before my mind has really caught up. Only Beau has the time for relaxing baths, and heavens forbid she ever realises it has to be paid for. I bang on Beau's door, it takes her ages to put all the make-up on that she doesn't actually need. She has the time, but doesn't need the make-up, whereas I need a little helping hand from its application, but don't have the time; another of life's little jokes. "Beau, time to get up love" I say as I open the door. Putting on my happiest voice in tribute to

Logan Coss, I sing "... and, it's a super lovely day out here today and you're going to be fabulous".

" Aww, Mum, will you do us all a favour and stop listening to that dick of a DJ!" Beau replies from under her duvet.

"Only if you're good, so that'll be never then eh? Come on, time to get up. I need to get ready and head off, I'll be back after you've gone."

"Okay, okay," comes the surly response.

I am ready in record time, no need to worry too much about my appearance, all I do is race from house to house helping the old folks the agency sends me to look after. Carer; general overlooked dog's body more like. No-one really appreciates having us cooking and preparing their meals, bathing them, cleaning them, cleaning up after them, chatting to them, caring for them and just being there for them when their families can't, or won't. Some are so lonely it is heartbreaking, others so nasty and rude that I can't wait to get out of their homes, even though I know they can't help it. After a lifetime of disappointments it is not surprising most of them are bitter and resentful I guess.

Rushing to put my shoes on, I hear "Mum, can you give me a fiver, I need it for lunch and bits today." I get my purse from my bag and look inside, I know what is there, you always do when there isn't much and every penny counts, but my heart sinks all the same. Six pounds thirteen pence to my name until tomorrow; great. "Of course love, it's on the side by your keys. Have a nice day sweetheart, loves ya."

Before I've even got to the front door, Beau's bedroom door opens slightly and I dread what is to come.

"Mum, I forgot, I need some money for dinner later as I'm going round Hollie's. Can I have another fiver please?" she shouts from somewhere behind the opening, not even coming out.

My heart sinks, I can't, I have nothing more to give, whatever I have is never enough, typical. Even when I go without, it is not enough to give her what she wants, but it is always just enough to make both of us unhappy; no winners here, again.

"Sorry love, I haven't got any more, can't you eat here before you go?"

I know what the answer is before she speaks; she's fully awake now and getting agitated as she wants something and feels it her right. "Come on Mum, pleeeease, don't be stingy, you know that means I'd have to walk for ages and it's not fair. Come on Mum, just another fiver, that's all I need?"

Need, what is it she really needs I wonder? She needs lots of things, a future, a career, to find something that makes her happy, contentment, dreams, commitment, lots of things she can't see and has no desire to see. You think everything will come your way when you are young and everyone thinks they have rights, rights to whatever they want, which is what others have, but what they want isn't always what they need. Bracing myself I say, "No, sorry love, you'll have to make the fiver last or eat here first. Sorry, have a nice day though and call me later. Loves ya!"

I try to keep upbeat, but it is difficult, especially when you hear a sixteen year old moaning "Fucksakes, that's so fuckin' unfair…" as you walk out the door to go to your crap job. If it wasn't so depressing, it would be funny, such a nice way to be bid farewell, from the person I love most in the world, before setting off on my way to another shitty day, full of having to do shitty tasks that no self respecting teenager would ever demean themselves to do. All to get hardly enough money to get by on and certainly never enough to meet the needs of an ungrateful sixteen year old. Is she ungrateful, or is it just that she doesn't understand, can't understand? To her, life should be fair, with enough for everyone, she has rights, she deserves that money, why shouldn't she, others have, so why shouldn't she have the same? Perhaps I should have left her the other one pound thirteen pence; I feel a bit mean as I could do without really.

    I get to the basement, collect my bike and take it out the side entrance, down the stairs and off to my Liverpool Street appointment. A miserable and ungrateful old lady I have to see three times a week first thing; checking she is OK and then cleaning her up and giving her breakfast before leaving her in her sitting room until the lunch time support arrives. It is really not very pleasant, any of it; you need a tough stomach for some clients. Can't be too choosy though, I just need to be grateful for having a job, if I wasn't lucky enough to be able to rely on this, there is no telling what we would do. Then there really would be arguments, well, more arguments. At least after this first one I have a thirty minute break where I can come home and tidy up before the next job. Right, let's get this day going…

An hour an a half later, I am home. It really wasn't good today, poor dear needs to be in a home with the full time help she really needs, a need that should be a right, but won't be met. It was not very pleasant at all having to clean up after her like that, but it wasn't very nice for her either, she gets so embarrassed and seems so very defenceless and lost, poor thing. She soon turns into a sharp mouthed old cow though when she is dressed and waiting for her breakfast though; it is funny how people's moods change depending how vulnerable they are feeling. Thirty minutes to clean up the breakfast bits and give the flat a quick tidy as Beau doesn't see what needs to be done, either can't or won't. I can't really remember what I was like then, so I don't know. Another of life's little tricks. As adults we probably just forget what it was like when we were growing up, so we are either too lenient, always giving our kids the benefit of the doubt and letting them get away with things we are not quite sure whether we did or not, or we are too strict, perhaps expecting more than was ever expected of us; where is the middle ground and who knows what fair really is? Bless her, she has a lot on her plate growing up, trying to decide who she is and endeavouring to define the person she will be and who she wants others to see. Poor kid, she just needs to get off that phone of hers, do some homework and focus on what she wants to do when she leaves school, but she seems to just wants to have fun, have it all, with no commitment. Kids just don't seem to commit to anything these days. I wonder if I did? They seem to just want everything and think they will just get it as they deserve it; perhaps they will, perhaps they won't. They should at least try a bit more shouldn't they?

Right, time for St John's Close, a nice easy number to clean the house of a lovely chirpy old couple who are just a bit to doddery to do it themselves; it is one of the nicest jobs I have, just a bit of a trek to get there. Getting the bike, I bump it down the steps for the second time today, this does get a bit dull, but life has pattens and routine and some days the seeming monotony just wears you down more than others. Today is one of those days and I can't wait for it to end. How to escape the hamster wheel of life? I had to make a meagre packed lunch and fill an old plastic bottle of water for lunch as, obviously, I don't have money for anything else and just need to make do. Just as I am putting it in the basket, I notice a tortoise shell cat I haven't seen before just staring at me from its spot by the fence where it is sat. It looks such a soppy thing, just lazing there as if it is lost and unsure, just hoping for some attention and love. I stare at it, you can never tell with cats, as cute as it looks, it might be sizing me up as a meal, I think I am a bit too big for the little fella, but naughty torties have different ideas to the rest of the cats I meet. Just as I am thinking this, a motorbike starts revving and both the cat and I jump from the suddenness of the loud noise; by the time I look up, I can just see its brown, black and white tail darting through the fence and into the park. I hope the poor thing is OK, cats have such unpredictable lives. It's funny what you see, how life constantly changes; there is always something else to see, but only if you have the luxury of time.

Time, yes, what a luxury. A luxury I don't have, on-on.

Hector - Money Matters

I have had a lovely morning, got up and dressed with plenty of time, feeling good after a night off the drink for once. It is a real treat to have a quiet night in every now and again, just a bit of tv and early to bed; alone for once, haha. Parties and meals out are all well and good, and I would go mad without a good social life, but we all need to recharge out batteries some time. Strong double espresso from the machine to get me going before a long lovely power shower, I do love the under floor heating and am glad I had it put in; cold feet in the morning is just too much hardship to ask anyone to put up with. It was intolerable before, but much more bearable now.

Cleaned and preened, I get my battle gear on; Gieves and Hawkes suit, crisp white shirt, pure like me, all finished off with clean and shiny Buckinghamshire brogues. All as it should be. Getting ready reminds me I ought to pay Sandy, perhaps even leave her a note as well, she is doing a good job keeping the place tidy and everything in order. I have no idea where she gets my clothes dry cleaned now, but it is much better than before with crisper collars on my shirt. Limp collars are most unsatisfactory. I admire myself in the full length mirror in my wardrobe; I feel good and I know I look good. Trim and dapper, but I am missing something and just need to finish the look off. I walk into the bathroom and splash a generous portion of my new aftershave into my hand, rub them both together and liberally splash it all over my face. I am not completely sure about the smell to be honest, but it was the most expensive in the shop and they assured me it was on trend and a lovely fragrance for others to smell.

Perfect, I am more than ready to make another killing today. I decide to get a latte and pain au chocolat from the little deli round the corner; lovely coffee, lovely pastries, really lovely waitresses, and waiters too if I am honest. A good start to the day, and if I didn't, I would have prepare something for myself and that would be rather dull.

Just as I am leaving, I get a text from my brother, Caesar. It annoys me as he, or more likely his interfering wife Kristie, is trying to set me up with another one of their friends: 'Dinner Thursday night bro, just a few friends coming, mostly couples, so K has invited Chantel from her yoga class. Apparently fit as, fancy it?'. Chantel, sounds classy, but I wish they would leave me alone, I know they mean well, but they just can't stop trying to help everyone, any one. Stop it, sort yourselves out and get your career back on track Caesar old chum before match making if you want my advice.

I shut the door as I am typing my reply, thinking how I can turn them down again without hurting their feelings. I need to be careful here, no need to turn this into anything it is not; as much as I hate their interference, I know their hearts are in the right place. Bloody Caesar, social worker extraordinaire, always looking for a good cause, always looking to give his advice and help. He believes everyone deserves help, and money is just a means to an end, a means to make the world a better place. He has lost the plot! I don't need their help and he would be better off trying to put his efforts into doing something useful and making money for a change, rather than giving it away willy nilly. He's changed, ever since he hooked up with Kristie and lost his focus a bit, he used to be fun and know how to have a good time, but that was before he got all loved up and serious about life.

I am just writing my reply when I hear a funny little sneezing noise… I glance up mid text to see a cat sneezing of all things, how weird. It is just sat there in the mud sneezing. Cute in a way, but I hate cats as they are always shitting in someone else's garden. They never seem to shit in their own garden and the bloody park is not big enough for them either apparently, much better to shit in someone else's garden. The amount of times I have seen them in mine is incredible, and disgusting. At least I don't have to sort the mess out, thank heavens for Jim, he seems happy enough to sort the garden out for me for a few quid each week. I am glad for people like him, he may be old, must be nearly seventy I guess, but he still knows his place and is grateful of a little extra money. Mind you, the cats are the least of the problems in the park, if it is not full of lazy chavs taking another day off work, it is full of drunks drinking their benefits away or the homeless; it is creepy that they are allowed so near to our homes, it shouldn't be allowed. I am sure they just try their luck to get people to give them money with the 'oh look at me, I'm so poor and helpless, it's not my fault I can't be arsed to get a proper job' look. No way, I've got better things for my hard earned money thank you. Speak to Caesar, he is a soft touch, in fact, go and bloody well sleep outside his house and see if he likes it!

The cat is behind me, probably already making a beeline to crap in my garden, I continue on my way up to the deli whilst texting my brother that 'I'd love to, what time?'. I walk in and see a couple of good looking girls behind the counter, I know Gilly but the other is new, and Josh, a very good looking barista; perhaps I will stay a while as I might catch their eyes, in a good way. I finish texting as I enter, I feel comfortable in this place as it is full of nice people, my people; relaxed, good coffee and expensive enough to keep out the wrong types. No chavvy mums with their screaming kids drinking coffee they shouldn't be able to afford, but can somehow.

"Hey, hi Gilly, how's tricks?" I ask, god I would love her for a night at mine.

"Morning Hector," comes the cheery reply, "usual?"

"Yes please, but can I have it in a take away cup as I've got a lot on. Oh, and a pastry please."

"Of course, take a seat and Sam will bring it over."

"Thanks".

I take a window seat and pretending to check my emails, half looking out the window to see who is about and half checking the staff. It is the best thing about city life, good looking people, everywhere! You have just got to find them amongst the dross and drop outs. The best ones are always the good looking bored ones, and there is always plenty of them, just looking for company and a quick fix of fun.

"Here you go," says Sam, placing my latte down, "and

apparently you like pain au chocolat with it?" she says placing it down as well. "Absolutely," I reply, smiling into her lovely hazel brown eyes; she would do very nicely, would probably love my pad, help me waste an hour or two.

"Gilly knows me so well, I'm such a man of routine," I laugh, "it's Sam isn't it?"

"Yes, I've only just started," which obviously I know.

"I'm Hector, I live just down the road, over there." I say, pointing vaguely towards the nice side of the park. Before I can follow up, she has turned her back and is heading towards to the counter; obviously she doesn't know the area, silly cow, full of herself, probably has nothing and never will. Oh well, maybe I will try again a bit harder another day, it is always worth being pleasant and keeping options open, just in case I am at a bit of a loose end.

I finish my pastry and then head off, saying "Thanks everyone," as I go, making a special effort to raise my cup and with my best smile say "great coffee as usual, cheerio" to Josh. There is another one I would welcome back to my place without a second thought. In fact, I would welcome anyone, within reason, just to make life that little more bearable for a while. I know I have a nice pad, I have spent a fortune decorating and furnishing, or rather getting people in to do it, but it is just a bit… I can't quite put my finger on it, but then it comes to me, it is just a bit lonely some times. Life is a bit dull without anyone to share it with, not someone to show it to, but someone to really share it with, and my feelings and thoughts, indeed my soul. The thought of furnishing the place makes me remember Becca, my interior designer, now she was fun, we even went to the Maldives together for a little break; good while it lasted, but she turned out to be rather dull and tedious after a while.

I skirt round the top of the park. Just ahead, I can see that young mum sitting on the steps of her crappy flat again. I see her a fair amount, coming and going with her young kid, sitting on the steps vaping, stroking a black cat — are they lucky or unlucky, I can never remember? It is funny how some people enter your life more than others; some people live near you and you never see them, like my neighbours, whilst there are others you notice only once, and fleetingly at that for some reason but then never again, and a few, like this pretty filly, who you always seem to see. It is either fate or simple routine, your lives become unintentionally intertwined yet you may never really acknowledge or talk to them, you just see them. She is rather delightful to be honest, often laughing and joking with her young lad, who seems to wear some very strange outfits, or just smiling. What has she got to be so happy about I wonder, she lives the wrong side of the park to have money and the flat looks like a bit of a shit hole to be fair? She is a pretty little thing though, obviously hasn't had too hard a life; effortlessly pretty actually, one of the few who doesn't need make-up, clothes or jewellery to pull it off. In fact, her clothes are rather tatty too, so it is really quite amazing that she can look so good and happy. I wonder if she is married, it is such a shame the good ones always seem to be taken, and especially sad when they hook up with someone who can't really provide; if only we had met a few years ago. She reminds me a bit of Tammie, now she was delightful and quite good fun too; a model from a good family in the Czech Republic. Great looking girl who knew how to party, we had a right hoot when we went skiing in 1850 earlier this year. Good fun for a holiday, but it all got very dull very quickly after that; she always needed this, must have that and couldn't leave without make-up being slapped on. A great girl to have on your arm, but quite annoying and strangely rather plain when she hadn't made herself up. Great fun in bed though, shame she wasn't really my type.

I walk directly in front of her flat, drinking my mediocre coffee as I go; can't do anything other than sip it as the dick who made it, good looking as he is, must have boiled the bloody milk. I wonder if she is watching me, wishing she had made other choices when she was younger, wondering what I would be like, how much she would enjoy it? I decide I would love to find out more about her and surprise myself when I realise I am attracted to her, even though she has nothing, but I find myself very attracted nonetheless. Even more surprisingly, I realise I would like to chat, take her out, get to know her; weird.

I carry on towards the tube station, musing about what could be and why I am thinking this way, I automatically speed up a bit as I pass the crap shops selling crap things for crap people; cigarettes, scratch cards and cheap booze. I positively rush past the betting shops, where the dregs of society go to spend their benefit money; lazy bastards, too lazy to work and adding nothing to society. God, there are some awful people round this area, really bloody awful; cheap barbers, crap coffee shops, fast food joints and kebab shops selling lukewarm tasteless chicken and meat that is made from the scrapings; lips, arseholes and eyelids in a wrap. Delightful. It is all rather squalid, I wish the government would do something, these people need a good sharp shock. They have no idea what hard work is, what it means to be committed, do your bit, have a part to play. It is all relaxing, boozing, moping and existing for these people. Get a life; in fact, call Caesar, he would be here in a flash and give you enough money to get pissed for a few hours, that is always the answer. At least there are some nice places nearby, it is not all bad round here and luckily these losers know to stay away from our part of town.

I get to the tube, throw my coffee in the bin, and dive in; an unfortunate leveller of life this, everyone together. Jam packed going down the ski slope steep escalator, the air getting warmer with every metre, all to get on a carriage that is haemorrhaging people, to gently rock our merry way into town, and work to do our bit and make some money. I might have a few drinks after work, catch up with the lads and see who I can pick up for later, I can't spend another night by myself in that soulless house of mine. I need a holiday, I work far too hard and my life has become mundane and monotonous, full of stress and loneliness that drives me, all to often, to seek someone out to spend the night with, someone, anyone. It is easy in the city, too easy, there are so many of us lonely people; we catch eyes, chat, flirt and have some meaningless chit chat before having an evening of mutual, but meaningless, pleasure. It seems so satisfying in the moment, yet so utterly soul destroying afterwards. Flirting, flattering and having sex is easy, anyone can get intimate with someone if they really want too, so we all put our game faces on and get stuck in; it isn't really us and I think we all know that. We would all like to be better and happier people really, but how? The only criteria are to be good looking and available, whether boy or girl doesn't really matter, it is just a short term fix to help us forget life. We hide our true selves, no in-depth discussions, certainly nothing that will be remembered, and nothing, ever, too meaningful. A fun, yet empty, satisfying, but ultimately unfulfilling night of pleasure to keep the loneliness at bay, at best; at worst, a life ruined with regrets. God I need to sort myself out and find someone that matters, that is the aim of life, find someone or something to care about rather than just having sex, working and partying. I just need a chance in life to help me find the right person.

Ellie - Perceptions & Realities

I dash out of the flat as I'm running late, running late, but looking good. My hair is looking lovely and straight this morning, I'm really pleased with it, it doesn't always work out how I want it, but that's because of the crappy straighteners I have to use. I'm worried I'm looking a bit orange today, perhaps I put a little too much fake tan and foundation on, but it should be ok. My lashes are well good too, new mascara that has an awesome brush that makes so much difference; I should have this more often, but it's so unfair that I never get enough money. Tia always has plenty of money for anything she wants, she's lucky, her parents love her; still, she is sweet and does lend me some every now and again. The others all have enough money too, I know Hannah has a little Saturday job, but that's just unfair because she only got it because her Mum knows the manager. I'd be much better at it. Ben and Jake both have paper rounds, seems like a thing kids should be doing as they're too old really, and I know they do feel a bit embarrassed about it when we take the piss, but then they just get on with it and are finished before anyone else is up and about, and they get paid fairly well. Luckily they're quite generous too. It could be worse, they all know I have it tough, no fault of my own, it's just difficult at home, it's just lucky I know how to make myself look good and am so funny as that hides lots of sins. Everyone lets you get away with more if you're pretty, everyone knows that, jokes are funnier, clothes more fashionable, everything is better; if you're not good looking, you have to try harder.

Better send a group chat to let everyone know I'm on my way, there's nothing worse than missing everyone. I need to catch up after all the gossip last night, so much going on at the moment, life's so busy. Roll on the weekend to get away from school and live life a bit, we're kids at school, or so they like to think, but we're not, we're all practically grown up now and should be treated like adults. We'll make a better go of everything when it's our turn than our parents did, they have no dreams, no friends, no fun. It's all so dull; dull jobs, dull lives, dull everything. And then they tell us we need to get a life and get off our phones; what on earth do they think the phones are for? Networking, socialising, pulling society together, sharing images, sharing jokes, having fun, being alive. The older generation just miss the point, just because 'in my day we'd spend our lives outside having fun and being care free' they think we should be like that. But it's different now, we're a connected society and you need to keep engaged 24/7 to keep up; just because they can't see it, they don't understand just how connected and engaged we are. One minute parents are telling us to be care free and the next that we ought to stop being so wrapped up in our own lives and start thinking about our futures as we won't get jobs if we don't study and without jobs we'll all be fucked. Yeah, right, they did really well didn't they? No money, no friends, no hopes, no dreams, and just spending most of their time being worn down by life. Phones and the internet are here to stay people, this is our life, our future and I think we're doing pretty well thank you very much. What do we need to worry about school for when we have the knowledge of the whole World available in our pockets? I will always remember something one of our teachers said about Einstein, which was that you should never waste time memorising things you can look up. Exactly! What do they think we'll be doing in the future, what they're doing? No thank you, no way.

Life's just different and they're out of the loop. If only they understood what the world is really like and that it's all about equality and rights these days , not persecution and knowing your place like it was when they grew up. I'm an adult, I have the same needs as them, after all I need money to look good and I've got to eat. I don't even get enough money to have many coffees at Starbucks for fucksakes, so unfair. Everyone else does, should I be left behind just because I don't earn at the moment, I will do and just need enough to get by, enough to get me on my way, wherever that might be.

'You ought to study' she says, 'what for?' is my standard response. Of course I know, but I don't want to just accept her points. 'So you can get a good job and have a future' is the answer I always get back. Future, what future, yours or mine? If you mean so I can live like you, making do, getting by; yeah, can't wait. But then I don't need to tell you what I do, I don't need or want to tell you my dreams, you'd just try and crush them, destroy them before they can grow and develop. My future is precious and it's mine; my future is for me to drive, not you to explore and criticise, from looking at a world you don't understand into a future that will leave you even further adrift and unsure. No, of course I study, I just study differently than you, if you did ever actually study that is. Why should it take us as long as it took you all to learn, we have technology to help us now, life has picked up a pace, so why can't you see learning has changed? I want to go to college, I want to learn photography, I want to be a photographer, help people discover the things they see but never *observe*;

capturing moments for eternity, capturing time itself. But you'd never understand that would you, everyone takes photos these days, everyone has a camera, so what's the point, that's a dead dream you'd say; yeah, according to you.

I rush down the street, school bag slung over my shoulder, to meet my friends at the gate to the Vic; same place every day. Meet up, chat about what's been going on overnight and find out who's made an arse of themselves, who's fallen out, who's out of favour. Lots to keep track of, laughing, scheming, plotting, living. Everyone's a bit morose today, there has been a fallout and it has split opinion. Max and Zoe are both popular and had been going out for a while, everyone thought they were a great couple. They split up overnight when it turned out Max had gone out with Caz, a right slut from our school. To make matters worse, they had an open fight and we all read the fall out. Max was then a right bastard and sent some pictures of Zoe to some of his friends, the boys, bragging and belittling his once love for Zoe. It wasn't very nice and no-one really got much sleep with arguments, accusations, tears and tantrums flying across the ethernet, hidden to anyone outside of our group, devastating and real to those of us wrapped up in it. Life's so unfair, Zoe was silly to send the pictures to Max, but everyone's done it before. No-one has been so publicly humiliated before though and it feels like life is now beginning to get a bit tougher, harsher than it was. Some people are starting to become more extreme than they ever used to be; life used to be just fun, now boys look for violence, some steal, some drink and look for trouble while you can see that others are starting to give up, smoking too much weed, looking to grow up and just move on from their lives. Sad.

It's Charlotte who notices as I arrive. "Hey, your hair looks amazing, where'd you get that colour, did you do it yourself?"

"Thanks," I reply, "yeah I did it myself last night, the dye cost a fortune and was a real pain to put on. I love it though!" I am beaming, pleased she's noticed and the others have too now. We chat a bit about the best way to colour hair, then we moved on to the bigger issues.

Charlotte, Hannah and I sit with Ben and Jake, how can we face school today when we know how much upset there will be? It'll be a day full of recriminations, hurt, anger, tension. We agree it's best to stay away, for the morning at least, which will be fine. We discuss the situation, it's a real mess and everyone is affected. I think Jake has seen the pictures of Zoe, but he at least has the good grace to say not; poor girl. A meaningless photo sent without thinking, but archived forever in the virtual world of life; a person becoming meaningless pixels, the pixels just being a picture to view fleetingly, forever spreading to more and more people, the person in the picture becoming less real and detached. They will never own their image again and will never know who has seen them at their most vulnerable and exposed. A photo sent without thought, all innocent enough at the time, but now meaningful in the consequences. We all sit and reflect.

"Max is such a twat," Hannah says and we all agree. "Look, Zoe's updated her profile," Ben says, "I wonder who she'll hook up with next?"

"Don't be such a dick Ben, she's been really hurt by that twat, he's a fucking moron for doing that," I say. "He only meant it as a joke El," Jake responds, "just chill. Look, Tom's been tagging again, look at this."

Before I can say what that twat Max did isn't fucking funny, everyone is looking at a Photo of Tom, next to another building with his tag on it, high up where no sane person would ever venture, you'd never get me up there. He's very brave, but it's all pretty pointless; he loves people knowing how courageous he is, it keeps him going ever higher, always taking more risks. He'll either eventually find what he's really looking for or it'll end up badly, all just for the thrill of getting his tag higher than anyone else's.

Now everyone is pouring over new photos, updated profiles and keeping abreast of life, moving on from poor Zoe, yesterday's humiliation for others, but still with a lifetime of regret and hurt to come for her. Everyone is chatting about anything of interest they find, the rest of us all following the trail on our own phones from the instructions given, racing from person to person, assessing lives, observing and commenting on everyone. No one is above comment, but it's all soon forgotten.

Ben starts smoking, I'm still not sure why he does this, it really stinks and I don't know how he affords it, perhaps his parents just love him more and give him more money. Ben's done it for ages, years, Jake's smoked for years too and even Hannah has been smoking for a while now. I don't see the point of it really and I'm sure they didn't at the start either. When we were younger, it was cool, fun and innocent, we'd all laugh when Ben learnt to blow rings of smoke into the air and I have to admit I found it clever at the time, but not now. Now, they smoke out of habit, it's who they are, probably who they always will be; I'm not sure what defines us, but it just happens. Without conscious thought, we seem to simply become who we are based on what we've done, not who we really want to be. Sometimes life takes over on autopilot, we're taken in the direction our life wants to go based on the trajectory of the past and rarely do we get a say.

I'm bored with the virtual world, so start looking around the park while everyone continues staring at their phones. Charlotte has just spotted an old photo of Zac from school when he was at primary, everyone is laughing thinking it's so funny that he was so puny and young; things like this are dynamite, worth storing for another time, funny as you like.

I'm looking at the sun streaming through the leaves of the overhanging trees, the dappled sunlight, the beauty of nature is mesmerising. It's one of the reasons I want to be a photographer, you spend time looking for a good shot, appreciating life around you, conscious of what's going on. The different shaped leaves, the sunlight that has travelled so very far, fighting it's way through the foliage to be stopped and create the ever changing shadows and shapes on the pavement. These sights are always there to be seen if you look, they're all around us all the time, but remain hidden to most. I take a photo on my phone as the colours and textures are beautiful. I look up and see another sight worth capturing, a slightly tubby black, white and brown cat, just sat there in the bush, watching us. I wonder if it's assessing us as readily as we assess everyone else. Perhaps it just wants a stroke. The colours contrast really well with the bush, with the sunlight just penetrating far enough to illuminate it. I point my phone, zoom in and take another photo, black and white this time, and am happy with the results and simplicity of the shot.

I'm not the only one to see the cat, Ben throws his cigarette down and throws an almost empty can of Coke towards it. The can hits the pavement in front of the startled poor cat, the dark contents spilling from the can on the pavement, which then clatters across the hard surface. The cat is gone in a flash, dashing across the path and into the bushes beyond, clearly afraid, it won't be back.

"Fucking hell Ben, you're such a fucking dick," I shout. "What?" is all he can say while shrugging his shoulders and smirking "It's only a stupid cat, what's wrong with that?"

"Oh, fuck off." Things are changing now, really changing, it's as though life knows we'll finish school soon and is ready to just spit us out; life is toughening us up, turning us into the people we'll be, do we have a chance after all? I wonder sometimes. Well, I don't have to sit here and accept it, this isn't who I want to be. "Right, I'm off to school, I can get there for the next period. Anyone coming?" I ask. Charlotte says she will, but the others stay on the wall and light up some more cigarettes just as we head off. It feels more of a meaningful departure than normal, I can't think why. It's not final yet, but I know the time is coming when we'll all depart from our childhoods for good, I just hope my dreams are given a chance. I don't want to have to give up just yet, I haven't even got going.

"Hey, El, are you still coming out later?" shouts Hannah.

"Duh!! Of course, fuck all at home to do," I laugh. "See youse all later!"

With that, Charlotte and I head off for school, we'll get a bit of grief for being late, but we won't be there for much longer so I don't mind.

Frank - Frustrations, Fortunes & Fun

There she is, what a beauty. Gorgeous, a real knock out.

The tortoiseshell cat from a few houses down often comes into my garden, she is such a lovely little thing. These are our favourite type of cat, Rowena loves them even more than I do; full of spirit, strong minded and fun, not soft and simple minded like some of the other ones. And they love the wool she knits with, too tempting for them to leave alone. It really likes that tuna I put out for it, it took a while for my little chum to find it, but the clever little thing did and now it always has a little look around the garden, just in case the tasty treat is there. Probably then goes off home to have its lunch; the thought tickles me.

I watch motionlessly by the window. I have been waiting for a while now, not really sure how long, but it seems an age, even for me. Rowena would kill me if she saw me here, in full view of the road, in my pyjamas, but I might have missed the cat if I had changed, it seems to take me longer than ever to get dressed now. I ache all over and find it all such a struggle. Still, no need to worry, it was worth it, my tiny friend has come now, enjoying her little treat she is. I am glad I made the effort but wish I had my camera to take a picture, tomorrow perhaps. I wonder where else she gets to? Same time everyday, more or less, before sauntering into the garden and having a mooch, looking for food.

I watch her wolf down the tuna chunks like she has been starved all week. It is a bit naughty really, Rowena will go mad when she finds out how much these little tins cost, but perhaps not, she has the softest heart of anyone I have ever met. Worth the risk though, to see my little buddy. She finishes eating, looks around and then the funny little thing has a drink from the old watering can, really leaning into it and getting her head right inside the hole in the canopy to get to the liquid. That water must be really old and smelly by now, I ought to put a bowl of fresh water out for her really. Finished, she looks up to find me, she sees me and I can sense she is saying thank you, although you never can tell with these ones, before turning her back and waltzing off like she owns the place.

It makes me happy to see the cat, well, to see anyone or anything, these days really. Still, best not to dwell, just be happy with what you have; don't dwell on the past, or worry about the future, just enjoy the present and plan as best you can, that is what my gorgeous Rowena always said. Bless her. How right she is.

I watch the cat walk to the end, hop on the wall and walk along out of sight, off for more adventures no doubt. I stand by the window for a while longer, envying the cat its freedom. I must get my camera ready for tomorrow, I just keep forgetting for some reason, I wonder where I put it, I am sure I had it recently. It really annoys me that I forget things these days, I know I am on the slippery slope and will probably think I am Napoleon soon enough, with hand tucked in my pyjama top when I look out on to the battlefield of life. I am sure my memory is getting worse, but you never really know, which is all rather ironic really. I do recall a programme on the radio where they said that older folks don't always forget more than the youngsters, it is just that we are more conscious about it and so beat ourselves up more. In turn, we remember forgetting more as the kids never worry about it in the first place. Who knows? All I know is I can't remember where I put my camera, I am sure I will remember later, just need to remember that I need to remember.

I realise I am still standing by the window in just my pyjamas, my legs ache and my back does too. I have a last look at my little garden and then walk to the front door to get the paper from the mat. I lean down and slowly pick it up, huffing and puffing all the way down and back up; life hurts these days, everything hurts, all the time. I walk back to the living room, my cosy little haven. I am fully aware that some would say it is a bit cluttered and that my things make the room look smaller, but I don't need much space and each bit of the clutter is a memory for me. I deserve to be able to indulge myself at my age, I have earned that right at least.

I head off to make a cup of coffee. It is the small things you miss as you get older, I used to love grinding coffee and making it on a stove top pot; years ago I found I couldn't unscrew the damn thing, so have to make do with instant coffee now. Such a shame. I head back to the living room and look for my glasses, which as usual are by the photo of my gorgeous Rowena, looking regal from her wooden side chair with an air of contentment and approval on her face. It always feels like she is looking over me and is here even when she isn't. I then sit and read the paper for a bit. I have never been very good at reading papers if I am honest; I read the headlines and skim read the first few lines of most stories, unless they really interest me. What can really interest me these days though? I am just an old man playing out the end of his days in a little house minding my own business; everyone sees me as an old man, and that is all. Most youngsters probably think I was born old and that they will stay forever young; haha, they'll find out, if they are lucky. Life is amazing, but cruel. The cruelty is that when you are young, you have fun but never really appreciate life as it is seemingly endless and stretches on forever, a year is a long time when you are young; when you're older though, you not only enjoy life, but really appreciate it, appreciate everything, as you know it is finite and like a vinyl LP that will end all too soon. A year when you are old flies by because it is only a small fraction of the time you have been alive; you slow down as you get older, but time speeds up. Funny really. I focus back on the paper as I don't want to get too detached from what is going on, but so much is alien these days. I try and keep up — politics is always politics, natural disasters are natural disasters, unfortunately religion has been a constant source of hatred, but the rest... well, I just don't understand it all to be honest. Everyone seems to expect everything, the social divides are increasing exponentially and technology is a complete mystery, albeit I know it is something that affects everyone and everything. I do try and keep abreast of current affairs, but it is just a bit much sometimes.

After having struggled to get ready, clean and out of my pyjamas, I put some bottles in the blue recycling bin; that's another thing that is baffling, why for so many years did we just have a dustbin but now need a whole collection of different coloured plastic bins that you can only put certain things in? The do-gooders say it is all about recycling and we need to all do our bit and should recycle to save the planet, the funny thing is that we always used to recycle even though we had dustbins. Televisions, radios, irons, everything used to get fixed, but that is obviously too difficult for the youngsters today, so they throw everything away when it is broken, but then think a few different coloured bins will make a difference, forgetting they are causing all the problems. It is like a Mensa test getting all the rubbish in the right place, well part of it at least. The other part is making sure I correctly out sort all my daily pills and take the right things on the right days, and only take them once; I rattle nowadays. I get to the end of the drive and realise I haven't got my coat and when I go back to get it, I realise I didn't have my keys, but luckily I had forgotten to lock the place up anyway. A few minutes later, and a few more self recriminations, I head off to the local shops to get some milk, tea, bread, cheese and tuna; life's staples.

The road is quite busy, but I don't mind as I like the buzz of the city, well, as long as it is not too busy. It is a beautiful day, the sun is shining and I can feel its warmth on my face; the air is crisp and I breathe as deeply as I can and enjoy the feeling, grateful that I can still get out and enjoy moments like this. If only I hadn't smoked for so many years, I would still be able to take deeper breaths, but back then it used to apparently be ok, nothing is ever as it seems and you need to be careful which experts you listen too. The advice you are given about so many things changes over time, it is all so confusing to know what or who to believe any more. I wonder if mobiles will be the modern day equivalent of smoking in the future — whether generations to come will be horrified at pictures of children with mobiles? That will be long after I have gone anyways.

Having got my shopping, I head home. It is always sad getting shopping for one, so little is needed, you don't need much; life is so much richer and fuller when there are two of you to share it together. Life is fun as a couple, it can be fun when you are left alone, but it is harder; it's more difficult to motivate yourself to do anything when you have no-one to share the experience with. I walk up my garden path, put the shopping inside and then get the cat's bowl ready to wash it in preparation for tomorrow. After I have headed inside, I make a cup of tea and then go back to my chair to read the paper; the news looks so familiar, it is the same every day.

After a while, I finish reading and decide to put a record on. Even now, I still cherish them, loving the artwork on the sleeves, the static hiss when you get the vinyl out of the cover, and the slight crackle when the needle hits the grooves of the record. I am proud of my hearing, everything else may be wearing out, but my hearing is OK for now. Music is the key to the soul, so much beauty captured in a timeless manner. I can get lost in it.

In fact, I do get lost, and find myself waking up to the rhythmic clunking of the needle at the end of the disc. I must have nodded off again, but why not? I don't sleep very well at night, so it is only right that I have little naps during the day to keep me going. Another old jazz classic has come to the end of the line unnoticed; similar to my own ending perhaps?

I indulge in the second side and manage to stay awake, focusing on the cascading sounds of the trumpet and piano in a beautiful embrace and the saxophone towards the end. It reminds me of a jazz club in Monaco, a lifetime ago; fun, champagne, glitz and Rowena. Every memory of any value has a hook into Rowena, she was my life, is my life. Love transcends the physical and she is still with me in my heart.

Right, enough of this. I have a quick cheese sandwich to ease my rumbling stomach before I wrap up and head out into the back garden. I may not be as active as I used to be, but I still pride myself on the garden. It has got me through some dark times, a constant companion that is forever changing, but always helps ground me in the present. It is getting wilder now that I can't really manage it by myself anymore, but it is a good look I have got going here as I do enough to keep on top of things in a way that makes it looks more natural than manicured. How I miss the feel of the earth between my fingers and in my hands, really connecting with nature. I would love to get stuck in if I could, but it is just too much of a struggle nowadays to get down and weed, let alone getting back up afterwards. The best I can do is collect up some of the debris, tidy a few bits up, water a few plants in the summer and feed the birds. I have got quite a collection of little friends that I have collected over the years, including a brave little Robin who hops around next to me chattering away. No fear, just companionship, he always makes me smile. There is a blackbird too, always waiting for a sliced apple, it knows I am a softie and will always have some around.

A garden is a great place to centre ones life; growing, living, dying, the eternal cycle. I would be lost if I didn't have my little garden with the beautiful roses and the bench under the beech tree, which is my favourite spot to sit and while away the day with a nice cuppa, when it is warm anyways. I am sure the days are getting colder now though, but that could probably just be due to my blood thinning as I get older. I'm just an old person now, or that is what people see when they look at me. They don't see a man, or someone who has lived, they just see an old man, someone who is fast approaching the end of their days. It's funny how you are perceived when you're old, you pass the point of being seen as a person with feelings of joy and happiness, oh, you may have memories, but that's all; no real value. Just a 'nice' old chap who is a bit eccentric with his life, which is visible for all to see in the wrinkles on your face; every line telling an unknown story. I know my house is probably dusty and smelly to anyone else if ever they were to visit, I know I have probably got hairy ears and stains on my clothes, but one of the good things about getting old is your eyesight gets poorer so you don't notice, so there are some benefits!

Right, I had better get on. Now, there was something I wanted to find, what was it…?

Sophie - Laughter, Loneliness and Life

Here he is, the love of my life bursting into the room, all energy and youth, happiness and fun. Boundless enthusiasm and a real love for life, who could ask for more? Such a good looking chap, but then I guess Mothers are always biased, meant to be biased, but he is a beautiful boy. Just like his father, good looking, loving and kind hearted to the core.

"Mummyyyyyyyyyyy," squeals Luke as he runs in to the bedroom. "Can I wear my spiderman to the party today, pleeeeeeeeeease?" He is such a happy kid, one of those people who has the gift of making others smile; not old enough to be wrapped up with insecurities or worries, just genuinely happy.

"Hey Luke, what a surprise! Didn't we talk about being just a tad quieter in the mornings?" I laugh as he jumps onto the bed. "Of course you can, if you can find it. But you do know the party isn't for ages yet don't you?" I reply. I can tell by the even wider smile that he has already found it and time is no issue, the party is today and that is all that matters. Another teacher training day put to good use. He hops off the bed and starts rushing out. "Don't forget to clean those teeth first," I shout after his disappearing form as it disappears round the door.

"Okaaaaaay!" is his response; no doubt he will forget and I'll have to remind him again.

Another morning waking up in bed, alone. Will I ever get used to it? Four years now, four long years without a cuddle from the only man I have ever truly loved. I still sleep on my side of the bed, still feel for his warmth in the middle of the night, am still shocked by the coldness and emptiness of the spot he used to fill. Every day I wake with the duvet still smooth over his side, I can't sleep like a starfish and spread out, it is still his side after all. My heart was broken, is broken; a gut wrenching inconsolable loss that is physically painful. At the start, the only thing that got me through each and every empty day was Luke, poor Luke, two years old and without a father. A father who was, is, an amazing person who will never be there to help and guide the son he loved as he grows up. A destiny unfulfilled, and for what? For what in-fucking-deedy. Such a terrible and tragic loss for all of us. Lee was my soul mate, my husband and my best friend. He is Luke's father and was meant to be his loving guide through the ups and downs of life, his advisor, his friend, his guardian, but no, all gone forever.

I put a smile on my face as Luke bursts back in. "Da-daaaah!" he shouts; spiderman with a little accessory round his neck, an old fake pearl necklace. "Wow, what a glamorous superhero," I laugh. He always breaks me out of my melancholy, he is good for me and we are everything to each other. He races back out and, alone again, I get out of bed, pull the duvet over and straighten it out with my hand, lingering over Lee's side. I get dressed in yesterday's clothes and head downstairs; some people like dressing gowns first thing in the morning, I like to get dressed, but not ready. It makes me feel more alive and alert, ready for breakfast and the day to come.

Downstairs, we have breakfast. Obviously not together, that would be too much to expect from an ever-so-excited superhero. Muesli and a coffee for me at the table and chocolate spread on toast for Spidy in front of a blaring tv; another children's tele special early morning 'drive-the-parents crazy' cartoon all full of colour and noise. It keeps him mesmerised while he eats his toast though, the party momentarily forgotten as he is totally absorbed in the excitement of it all. Missing the start is no problem with these programmes, they don't have a plot, it is just digital ecstasy for young minds; psychedelic. I sit for a while and just watch him, the light from the screen reflected on his transfixed little face. Perhaps I should wean him of his early morning tv fix, but I can't bring myself to do it. He will have enough battles in his life without them starting at home before he is even seven. Friends say I indulge him too much, but I don't think so, we just make life as fun as we can. We have already had enough heartache to last most folks a lifetime and I know Luke misses his Dad too, even if he never really knew him and can't understand it fully yet. You can sense a loss sometimes without knowing exactly what the cause is.

I just finish eating when the cat flap clatters and in pops Wilma; black, sleek and looking quite pleased with herself. The cat that got the cream I guess, probably pinching food from elsewhere again. She wanders under the table and rubs up against me so I can scratch her ear, she likes that, always has. It is good for both of us, she purrs contentedly and I get pleasure from the contact and feeling of love. We got Wilma once things started to settle down after what happened with Lee. I was far from fine, but wanted to have as normal a home life as I could for Luke and to start to get on with normality, whatever that is. Black suited my hidden mood, and when I saw the little bundle of black fur running around the pen with the other kittens, I knew she was the one for me. We named her Wilma because Lee always loved the Flintstones for some unknown reason. We'd spoken about getting a pet for a while; he was a cat person from childhood and loved their independence and character, whereas I had always been a dog person, loving their loyalty and fun. As ever, I'd been unable to resist his charm and we agreed on a cat. So we got a black cat after he had gone, a cat called Wilma. I am sure he would find it funny when I had to call her, always putting a little bit of Fred-like emphasis in it when I did so, just because it made me smile. We have to do everything and anything we can to find happiness, especially harmless innocent happiness.

Wilma may be a cat, and a very independent cat at that, but she certainly has the ability to sense moods and be there when needed. Many a night, having put Luke to bed after a full and fun day, I have curled up on the sofa, put something on the tv that I never really watched, and sobbed my heart out. Wilma is usually a night cat, she sleeps soundly for most of the day, but then goes out for the night life, but when I have been low, she's sensed it and stayed in, been there for me. Before the sadness could ever really get a hold and fully grip me, there she would be, as if by magic, on my lap fighting for my attention and then purringly with that reassuring rhythm that relaxes the soul when it vibrates into you. Even more amazingly, she would stay, making me settle and focus on the outside world, her, rather than the inside, with my memories and the sadness that accompanied them. So yes, I love Wilma, she is a precious member of our small family; Lee was right to persuade me to get a cat that's for certain. Heaven knows what would have happened to me, and Luke, if it hadn't been for my

Wilma. To the rest of the world, just another cat, but to me, she is a life saver.

I am brought back to reality by yet another burst of laughter from Spidy, the cartoon makers are worth their weight in gold for making kids all round the country happy and content. Exactly how they should be.

"Luke honey, I'm just going out the front for a while. I'll leave the door open and will just be on the step, call me if you want anything, ok?" I say to the absorbed figure on the sofa. "Uh huh," comes the soft distracted reply. I grab my things, put on a cardie and head outside for my one vice in life; vaping. Perhaps a bit trashy, but certainly much better than smoking; I still feel ashamed that I smoked around Luke in the tough days, but I know we can't always think straight and sometimes need to do unpleasant things and just be a bit selfish to get us through life. I kicked the habit three years ago now, but can't stop the vaping, especially now I have found the cherry blossom vape, such a lovely taste and smell although probably more addictive than smoking was to be honest. Perhaps *they* put special chemicals into the liquid to ensure addiction?

I sit on the steps in the early morning sun and watch the busy world going by. As ever at this time of day, everyone is in such a rush. It is nice to observe life unseen and watch people go about their normal days. No-one takes any notice of little old me, they all have important lives to get on with, and as they go past they are all thinking about work, loved ones and their personal challenges and dramas. Everyone has problems, who is to say whose are significant and whose aren't; the seemingly trivial can be serious, the seemingly serious only trivial. Everything is relative. Lee and I never really argued, but there was one time when we bordered on a real fall out which all started because of a crumb on the table; it wasn't the crumb that caused the fall out, obviously, and I can't even remember what the issue was really about, but it started nonetheless because of a crumb. A crumb that it that moment seemed to represent so much more. Once we realised, we really laughed about it and made up instantly, what a great make up that was. Perhaps there is something in the belief you need a little fall out with loved ones every now and again, who knows.

Suddenly I am grabbed from behind, little arms grasping around me, a head on my back and hands squeezing me. "Saved by a super hero, at last," I say as Luke continues to hug. "What's the matter Spidy, all ok?" I ask. "Mmm-hmm," comes the little reply. After a while of heart melting hugging, he lets go. I momentarily wonder when the hugs will stop forever and wish he didn't have to grow up. I can't imagine my little boy growing into a teenager and then a man who leaves home. Will he be a surly adolescent with every day being a dreaded battle, or remain a loving and fun teenager? Will he be a man who always keeps in touch, or will he leave me behind and focus on his life to be? How will I steer him, how can I steer him, if only his Dad was here to help, then everything would be ok? Anyway, I am sure Luke will be lovely, he's such a good kid.

"Hey, come here you little horror, I've got something for you," I say holding my clenched hand in front of me. "What, what?" he says all excitedly; he falls for it every time and I can't stop myself from smiling. He stands in front of me and I say, "This!!" and grab him and then start tickling him remorselessly. I pull him tightly close and tickle him with both hands while he can't move. He wriggles and squeals with laughter trying to get away. "Come on Spidy, where's all your super strength gone," I say between laughs, all the time tickling. He has always been ticklish; ticklish toes and feet, ticklish tummy, ticklish back, very ticklish neck. I pick his top up and blow a raspberry on his tummy; he almost collapses with laughter. This is the best tonic ever and long may it last, we are both happy and smiling, lost in the moment, the busy noisy road with its cars, buses, bikes and people suddenly blocked out and forgotten. We are alone, just the two of us, completely focused and lost in our happiness. What more, apart from my Lee, could I ever want. How can I ever be sad when I have this bundle of energetic fun to love and be loved by?

Sensing he is running out of steam, and knowing it is going to be a long, hectic and eventful day for him, I let him finally wriggle free. I look up and see Wilma's little friend from next door at the end of the path watching us. Such a strange cat that one, it never comes into the garden, never seeks out attention or fuss, it is a real loner, emotionless. I am sure it must be different with Wilma, one way or the other. Luke runs inside to watch another cartoon and the cat walks off, so it is just me once again, with my cherry vape, the sun and my memories against the rest of the world. All alone, alone but happy; alone and incredibly sad. With one last puff, I head inside to get myself ready for the day. It is one thing sitting on the step while unwashed, it is yet another to venture outside and meet people.

Having had a quick shower, towel dried my hair and got dressed, I tidy up Luke's room. The magical world of a six year old, where things just happen. They come in to a room and it is tidy, but they don't realise, then within minutes, everything that was in a cupboard is on the floor, yet still they don't realise and when they get back, it is tidy again, and they remain completely and blissfully unaware. Things just happen and six year olds accept it without thought, but then again, why shouldn't they?

Luke is still engrossed in what must be his fifteenth cartoon of the day when I come downstairs. I leave him to it as it is a bit of a luxury for him having another day off school today and he will be running around with all his friends soon enough. Not being able to resist, I head back outside. Within minutes, I see Mr stuck-up-my-own-arse, as I like to call him, walking along with his artisan coffee in hand; suited and booted in a very expensive outfit today. Usually when I see him it is with an ever changing, but never quite totally different, young girl on his arm, chatting away, but not really listening, wearing combinations of nice clothes that he never manages to get quite right. He must have a huge wardrobe, probably in a big house somewhere, full of nice things that he never bothers to think about before he puts them on. What a jerk. I have no idea why I see him so much, or notice him even, but I do. He is alone today and I can see him looking at me out of the corner of my eye. It is creepy, just because he hasn't got someone with him for once, but I know I am not his type anyway, I have got baggage and no money. As he passes, I look at him; he is trim, I'll give him that, and he doesn't look too bad today. However, he has clearly got far too much money and not enough common sense for his own good…

It is nearly time for the party, so I start to get Luke ready. Initially he is not very impressed when told it is time for the tv to be switched off, until I say, "That's OK Spidy, we can stay and watch cartoons rather than go to that boring little party if you want? In fact, what a great idea, I might do a bit of cleaning, we can…"

"Nooooo, no, no, no," comes the panicked reply from a now very hyperactive six year old. "Pleeeease, I wanna go!" he shouts, now bouncing up and down on the sofa in excitement. "Okay, okay. I guess we can go, but only if you promise to be good and remember to take Harry's card and present."

A few minutes later, with the card and present safely tucked under the arm of a pearl necklace wearing Spider-Man, we head off, out the front door and over the road to walk through the park to the community centre on the far side. It is such a lovely place the park and is one of the main reasons Lee and I decided to settle here in the first place. Yes, the road can get busy, and be noisy, and yes the area can get a bit feisty now and again, but overall it is worth it. At times you are very much in the centre of a hectic, mad city, whilst at others it seems like you are on the outskirts of a quiet market town — albeit with the constant wailing of sirens somewhere hereabouts. The park is such a lovely place for Luke and his friends to play. Of course you have to be careful, but I am. We are both in good spirits as we head off. I am happy because Luke is; Luke is happy because he knows the party will be fun, with sufficient yummy party food to make him hyperactive and enough space at the hall to go crazy with his friends and burn off the excess energy. I know these things usually end in tears at the end of the day, but there will certainly be lots of fun in-between.

The park is fairly quiet today, just a few people walking dogs and some couples chatting as they meander slowly along the path.

I see a group of teenagers bunking school ahead, all sat on a bench smoking; my heart sinks, I know what is coming. I distract Luke by getting him to look for a fictitious dog at the other end of the park whilst I steer us to the far side of the path.

"Fucking hell, it's a gay spider man," one of the loathsome teenagers says, just loud enough for us to hear. "Haha, it's chasing that squirrel round the tree, can you see?" I say to Luke pointing. "I bet his mum needs a good length," says another, "I'd take her all day long," says another of the boys. I keep on laughing with Luke, just trying to safeguard his innocence in life for a while longer. Inside I am fuming, I would love to give that needle dicked git a slap, how dare he. Luke can wear whatever he likes. I am used to the teenage boys playing the rather dull role of saying what they would boastfully do to any woman, MILF or girl they see, in fact the only criteria for being commented upon is having a vagina. That is just boys I guess, wanking all night, probably whilst dreaming of their friends, and then bragging about what they would do to women all day; pathetic. I would like to see them talk like this if Lee was here, but he isn't, so they can and there is not much I can really do about it. I am always cautious and wouldn't antagonise a group of teenagers, knowing I would either get attacked or have a brick thrown through my window at night; best just to leave alone and never let them have the satisfaction of a reaction.

Thankfully, I see the community centre and other mums arriving with their kids; none of the others are in fancy dress, but that won't bother Luke. He never seems to care what others do or think, he is a free spirit and that is what I love about him. No one bats an eye as he turns up in his outfit, it is just what Luke does.

As soon as we are outside, he instinctively releases his grip on my hand and charges in, all giggles and screams, the party has started and he is going to wring every bit of fun out of it he can. Luckily, he has some really lovely friends, it is just such a shame their mums are a mixed bag. It's not that they are unpleasant, any of them really. It is just that there are certain cliques, which mainly seem to align to which side of the park you are from. Sad really as the kids have no perception of wealth, they are just friends and don't care whether you have got a big house or a little flat. Some of the mums do though, it was one of the inevitable questions at the start, luckily, we are from the middle, so are able to get on with most of them, yet not really accepted by anyone. I think I am given the benefit of doubt because of my situation. I never talked about it at the start, but there are always questions and comments and sometimes Luke will mention something about the Dad he never knew that piques curiosity. Eventually, I did become more open about it, but then it becomes everyone's business and a simple gossip item for a slow news days. The single mum no more, there are plenty of them, no, I am the widow and even more excitingly to some, a war widow. A person with a background none of them have ever had exposure too, a tragedy they have only ever read about over their cornflakes or seen on the news. Their very own pet war widow, poor, poor me.

"Oh sod off," I used to want to say to them all, scream to them all, but I didn't as we live here and this is our home and I need their acceptance. So I just get on with it, tolerate their falsely sympathetic sad looks whenever they remember and just get on with things.

It has been four years now, four long years since I had two men in suits that I didn't know turn up at the door of the flat that Lee and I had bought ready for his new life. A flat we had bought just before he went on what was to be his last overseas tour before leaving the Army; it was indeed his last tour, but not in the way I had ever considered outside my nightmares. I knew as soon as I saw them on the doorstep, knew my soulmate had been taken from me, knew I would never know the sound of his soothing voice again, knew I would never feel his sweet touch, knew my Lee was gone. Forever. Once inside, they said I should sit down, but I couldn't; I couldn't sit when I knew they were going to change my life forever. Forever is such a long time and I would never, ever, see my Lee again. He was gone, had been fatally shot was all I took in, the rest of the details were a blur. Part of me died too that day, listening to the suited men who had gently entered our home before violently ripping my life apart with their news. My life became snippets of news in the papers after that; another tragic loss, another sad ending, another young woman made a widow before her time, another child without a father. I thought I could die, should die, would die — from grief, heartache, emptiness and loss. Mine and Lee's families were amazing and got me through the immediate trauma, but it was Luke who saved me — if it hadn't been for Luke, and Wilma, I have no idea how I would have coped.

    I'd had to start my life again. A cliché to many, but try it, it's hard. I didn't have any friends in the area as we had just moved here with dreams of the friends we would make together. I didn't even have a job at the time, so there was no-one apart from family to help me, but even family leave eventually as they can't stay forever. When the last person left and shut the door, I was truly alone, it was just me and Luke against the world. So, I did the best I could, I joined the local Mother-and-Toddlers group, playgroup and then got a job as a teaching assistant at Luke's school when he started Reception. He is my focus, so the job fits around his needs. We don't have much, but what do you really need other than just enough, especially when you have love?

I come out of my daydream, or living nightmare I guess, to find I am in mid conversation with Rosanna, one of the more well to do airs-and-graces mums here. She means well, but I can't stand the look of pity in her eyes when she tells me I need to find a new man and have some fun. She is one of those people who wouldn't be able to survive by herself, having to be independent, having to work and not being supported by a rich husband. Some people just miss the point of life. However, I know she means well and agree to go for a girls' night out with some of them in the near future.

It will be excruciating, but I know it is time to move on. I don't want to, but know I need to else I will end my days as an unloved old spinster. Time moves on and everything changes eventually.

Beware Bananas

I swear that bloody cat is going to get it. I can't believe she got me again, I am usually made of tougher stuff than that. I am as brave as they come normally, perhaps I'm just a bit under the weather? It is probably because my strength is starting to fail from these bloody awful biscuits I am fed ever day. That's all I can put it down to. Wilma must be laughing at me now, scaring me in the night, again, getting me told off, again, and shitting in my plant pot, again. It is a sodding disgrace, that's what it is. You wait Wilma, you bloody wait.

I am up and about a bit earlier today, all agitated like a caged lion, a beast looking for a fight. I pace up and down and scratch against the side of the sofa, getting ready for the conflict that must be. The man sloth bursts in and annoys me straight away by rubbing my fur, not once, but twice; baaaad mistake buddy, not today. With a scratched hand for his efforts, he opens the door and sulkily heads off to make his morning coffee. I am free, there is no dilly dallying today, oh no. Today I'm out of the door in a flash, in hunter mode.

The first thing that strikes me is the stench. Wow, she really is a disgusting. I mask the smell somewhat with my own morning ablutions, hopefully one of the sloths will sort this all out later before I get back, else it will start overflowing. The second thing I soon notice is that it is a bit drizzly and chilly today. Reluctantly, and only because it is not ideal hunting weather, I decide to head back in for the warm patch on the sofa, not to sleep, but rather to plan my strategy. Which I am indeed determined to do, after a few more of those awful biscuits.

Damn, must have had a little snooze. Man sloth is dashing out moaning about the weather and I haven't even the chance to rub against him before he goes. I must be ill. The drizzle has stopped though and it is a bit warmer when I next venture out. Cherry vape flavour abuses my senses, distracting my intent scan of the area with its deliciously sweet smell. No, must focus. I see Wilma's flat mate standing on the steps, wrapped up, watching the world go by. Her annoying kid is nowhere to be seen, or heard, today thankfully.

I am just wondering whether I should go and return the favour to Wilma in one of her pots, when I start to think that I may have peaked too early today. I really need to get my act together. I stop my recriminations when, to my delight, I see a black figure in the bushes across the road. Right, no messing around, it is time for action!

'Prepare for some pain, you disgusting animaaaaal,' I roar as I leap down the steps, one at a time to prevent risk of injury, and dash across the road. Wilma hasn't seen or heard me as my scream is lost amongst the morning chaos and noise. I am just over half way across the road, focused on Wilma, when I know something is wrong. Very wrong. My mind speeds up and unexpectedly I start thinking much quicker than normal; I know something is wrong, but no idea what it is. Suddenly, I am conscious of what it is, I have broken my cardinal rule, doubly so. Not only am I crossing the road earlier than normal, but far worse than that is the fact that

I didn't look before doing so. My consciousness is racing, trying to process the facts and keep up with what I am looking at, what I am in the process of doing and what I have just thought about. I'm still looking at Wilma while these thoughts are whizzing through my brain, trying to fully understand the enormity of what I have done, and what I have risked.

Before I can do anything else, I sense movement to my left. I turn my head, shocked but knowing I have no one to blame for this but myself, and expect the worst. My eyes widen in terror and disbelief, my heart quickens, my shackles raise and life seems to slow down even more. I prepare to jump for all I am worth and my claws extend. Coming towards me, at a huge rate of knots, is a lady in a white coat, on a bike eating a banana that seemingly prevents her from grabbing the brake to stop. I register shock on her face, and start to think I am sure I know her ,whilst I freeze in mid motion; bloody hell, this isn't the time to start thinking about where I've seen her before, just get out the bloody way!

Just as my thoughts are transcending into action, I feel an excruciating pain in my side. Aaaaargh! I've been hit! As if in slow motion, I see the bike smash into me! The wheel thuds into me on my left side, the pain is immediate, intense and like nothing I have ever felt before. I know this is bad, very bad. My head is spun away from the lady as I am lifted up and then feel myself spinning through the air. I just know it, I am going to die, just my sodding luck. All because of bloody Wilma!

I see the grey sky above, the trees spinning upside down, people on the pavement looking on, the road beneath me and then the sky above again. I land on my back, my head hitting the kerb, and am in instant agony, a shockingly powerful, all encompassing and absolute pain stabs through my side, back and head. I lie there, sprawled on the hard surface, broken, vulnerable and in pain. The thought that this is most unlike me not being agile enough to land on my feet goes through my mind; oh sod off I tell myself. My next thought is then to get out of the road before something else hits me and it takes a moment to get my bearings. I am in pain and scared; my mind screaming to get away, run, my body not responding as it should.

Before I can fully register which way is safe, and whether I am uninjured enough to move, there is another crash followed by a scream. Despite the pain, I manage to turn myself the right way up, struggle up on to my jelly like legs, and crawl onto the pavement, narrowly missing being stood on by passing commuters who don't seem to even notice me now, seemingly just getting on with their oh-so-busy-and-important lives. I manage to make it across the pavement and limp through the fence to the relative safety of the park, where I collapse into some long grass. God I hurt.

Stunned, disorientated and in significant pain, I look up; my head is spinning, my side is excruciatingly painful and my head hurts. As I focus, I see even more devastation. The woman in the white coat is sprawled on the road, her bike to one side and the banana discarded, covered in grit by her side. Cars have screeched to a halt on either side of the road and there is a domino-like effect as the screeching quickly moves along opposite sides of the carriageway. Traffic has been suddenly stopped and soon horns start blaring. People go over and help the woman, she gets to her knees and is helped to her feet and then to the pavement; someone gets her deformed bike and gently leans it against the fence next to where she is lowered, people chatting to her and asking if she is all right. She seems dazed rather than hurt. Within a minute, she is left to herself and people move on and the traffic starts again as well. No-one pays any real attention, no-one really cares, no-one wants their day disrupted by a simple accident. Motorists give her a cursory glance as they continue on their way, some out of mere curiosity, others sympathetically and yet more just look annoyed at having been delayed.

No-one looks for me, no-one notices me lying next to the fence just the other side of her, cut and bruised, panting and shocked. No-one cares. Within moments, you would never know anything had happened. It is incredible, they really don't care; they are dead to the world, dead to each other, dead to anything outside their own little worlds. I am shocked, literally shocked and stunned, for so many reasons.

The lady in the white coat is pushing her bike back along the pavement towards the flats I now remember having seen her at before. I am glad she is OK as I know this was my fault. I was stupid, I could have been killed, could have got her killed by my stupidity. Regardless of all my self recriminations, I just can't really comprehend how no-one cares about me, or the lady on the bike, or anyone or any-bloody-thing for that matter. How can this be?

I am lying here in agony and so much pain that I can't pin point it to any one single part of my body. I can't even try to conceal myself in the way I normally would, I am suffering too much and too injured to care or be able to do anything about it even if I wanted to. Most people just walk on by, looking at their phones and have absolutely no idea I am here. Others do miraculously look into the grass and see me, but their eyes are dead and they just walk on, they don't care and there is no way they will get involved or help, after all it would delay them and disrupt their busy important days. They have got their own agendas to keep and aren't going to stop for anyone. Literally, no single person cares. Sad.

Just when I think things can't get any worse, I realise Wilma is stood right next to me, watching. She walks over, silently stands next to me, sniffs me and then licks the back of my head. Strangely, I don't detect and sense of triumph in her actions, but neither do I sense any sympathy, but there again, what can she do? I will be stuck here now until the traffic is much quieter, perhaps until it is night, that is if I can make it at all. I know there is no way I can get home in my current condition as I would never make it across death-road without being hit again and I don't think I could physically walk it anyway. I will be here until at least the night time rush has passed; the thought makes me shiver involuntary. Being in the park at night is my worst nightmare. No, I realise trembling uncontrollably, my worst nightmare is being injured and helpless in the park at night.

I lie here and just watch the world go by for a while longer, before painfully dragging myself slightly further into the grass, trying to make myself less of a target. I am powerless and open to attack now. Hurt, alone and stuck here until the demons come. I realise I am feeling tired and my eyelids get heavier. This isn't right. My mind screams at me to wake up, I suddenly realise I am dying. I am going to die in the most inglorious manner possible;

run over by a banana wielding lady and not having anyone help me. I still can't understand why no one would help me, why no-one cared. Is everyone really in this life just for themselves, completely insensitive to others' needs? It plays on my mind, perhaps this is all I deserve, after all, who have I ever helped? Conflicting emotions fill my mind and try to compete with the feeling of pain. Anger at the stupid woman who wasn't paying attention, annoyance at myself for being stupid enough not to look before I ran across the road, self pity for being stuck here in the park, fear at being helpless, sadness at knowing I am unlikely to see another day and sympathy for the world, there really isn't any hope left, for anyone. I fight the coming darkness for a while, but the blackness is coming, I can see and feel it. I feel tired, lonely, in pain and scared, at least the pain will go soon. I fight it until the nothingness comes for me, no longer caring.

Awareness slowly returns to me, but my mind is fuggy and I am unsure where I am or why I am here. All I know is that I am outside in the cold and damp; I am stiff and sore with my side, head and legs hurting. I have never felt so despondent or alone and I am hungry, very hungry. I feel damp grass against my face and hear a distant siren in the night sky, other than that, it is very quiet; quiet and threatening. The events of the disastrous day start to slowly come back to me and I can't quite believe something like this could happen, not to me. Things like this happen to others, you never expect to be the one in the accident, the one who gets hurt, the one people see hurt but then just ignore and walk past. A traumatic and horrific accident for me, just another insignificant and inconvenient occurrence for others. Even those few that did consciously witness the accident will have probably forgotten about it by now, while I am still in the middle of it all. Hurt, alone, outside, cold and vulnerable.

I start to remember what happened now and register where I am. I am not just hurt, I am hurt and still in the park, at night! Panic sets in, my breathing starts to become ragged and fast, I start hyperventilating, I am going to die! Suddenly, I sense a presence, something is next to me, lying next to me. Lying right next to ME! Fur on fur, the hunter and the prey, side by side, a predator has found me when I was exposed and unable to defend myself, bastard! The thing moves, but slowly and gently. I feel a warm wet sensation on the back of my head and then a nuzzling in my side, painful, but not aggressive. Wilma comes into view, I realise she has been keeping me warm. She must have stayed with me, looked after me, protected me, been there for me; my nemesis is here, my saviour is here.

Without malice, just sympathy in her voice, she says, "Come on, let's get you home silly."

With that, she nudges me again in the side and the pain encourages me, groggily and unsteadily at first, to my feet. Pain shoots through me like electric shocks with each painful step, but Wilma is right by my side, supporting me in her own way. "Don't worry, I'll see you back home ok," she says reassuringly. When we get to the fence, she dashes through, has a look round and then comes back to tell me it is clear. I move slower than a big bag of slow things, hobbling really. I may be beaten and dazed, but I am alive. Luckily, it is quiet and we are soon at the bottom of my stairs, I can see the lights on in the flat, which is unusual. I try to climb the step, but it is just too much; so near, yet so far. I slump down, exhausted and defeated. Wilma dashes past me and up the steps out of sight. Seconds later, I hear a scraping at the door and then she is dashing past me again, going back into the darkness of the park.

I can hear the door open and see shadows above. "Did you hear that?" says a male voice. It is my sloth man, I have never felt so happy to hear his dull voice. "What?" says female sloth, also outside now.

I shout for help, but my mouth is dry and it is barely audible, even to me. It is too much, I know I can't make it. Then, unbelievably, he is bounding down the stairs, I can hear him, hear my rescuer.

"Oh, bloody hell" I hear him say. I am carefully scooped up, almost reverently so, and carried upstairs. "Quick, help me," he shouts.

It is the last thing I hear as the calmness claims me once again. I fall asleep feeling happy and safe, it turns out that the people who share my flat aren't so bad after all.

Clare - Dreams, Escapes & Realities

Why is it that everything has to be a bloody battle? Kids seem to be different these days I am sure; we used to have dreams, whereas they have expectations. I would never have dared, or dreamt, of speaking to my Mother like that, if I had, I'd have gotten a back hander and put in my place. Perhaps Mum was just stronger and more grown up when I was a teenager than I am with Beau, perhaps it is all my fault? Perhaps I am just too soft, weak even?

Another day, another argument, another breakfast comprising of just an old banana on my way to the first job of the day. No lunch, as I haven't got any money, and just dinner by myself to look forward to this evening, again, in front of some shite on the tele. Great, life couldn't be better. I am not sure what is getting into Beau lately, her moods are up and down like a bloody yo-yo at the moment. Full of expectations, but without any of the unseemly or tiresome commitment that would usually go with them and just cramp her free will and style. In her eyes, she deserves everything, life is full of rights and so, quite simply, there shouldn't be any privileges. She deserves a Starbucks, she deserves lunch out with her friends, she deserves to have enough money for shopping trips, she deserves new clothes, a new phone, new camera, new laptop, new bloody everything. 'Aww, come on Mum, just a tenner, you know I'm going out tonight after school' was how this morning's latest delightful exchange started. All I did was say cheerio before going to get on my old bike and cycle to the next appointment, ready to clear up the latest nighttime accident for some poor old dear on Kennington Way. But no, no chance of a 'see ya, have a nice day' or 'loves ya' for me. A full on assault about money, about being a shit uncaring Mum, about having no idea, not caring, never having fun, being a sad loner who caused her Dad to leave. Great, thanks for making me feel even shittier than I did about an already shitty day Beau; nice one.

    Ten pounds poorer I set off, meaning that after the first few home visits I will have just broken even. I clunk my bike down the steps and take my ever so weary heart off to work; it is chilly today, my hands going numb as soon as I start peddling. I set off mulling over the argument, about whether I should have given her the money, money she doesn't value and has no idea what I have to do to earn. I could have told her how hard my life is, what I have to do to earn it, how ungrateful she is, how it breaks my heart that whatever I do, it is never enough, how she has the knack of making me feel even more like one of life's failures. I could have told her that her Dad left because he was a heartless and hateful crack-head, a good for nothing loser who used to beat me, hurt me, force me, and couldn't stand her crying. I could have told her that when he left, I pleaded for him to stay, hoping he would sort himself out and be there for her. I could have told her my heart broke when he left, my dreams of love gone forever. I could have said lots of things, but I didn't. I just took all she could throw at me, let her use me like life's punchbag for all the unfairness she feels, left the money on the side, and went to work. I can't cope with any more battles, I just want peace and a chance to be happy, time to relax. I know I have got to be careful what I wish for though, what have I got to look forward to really? A quiet flat with Beau grown up and moved on, with me unable to do the same; middle aged, no hopes, alone, useless.

    I need a holiday, somewhere hot and sunny, somewhere you can lose yourself and forget your worries, forget life's troubles and just be happy in the make believe world of some far off resort. I could imagine myself lounging by a pool, Beau at my side, the two of us watching to world go by, having private jokes about anyone who unknowingly catches our eye. Of course, I would need a holiday romance, who would dream of going on holiday without romance? The thought makes me smile, as if I would ever have enough spare cash for a proper holiday, or be lucky enough to find romance! As if anyone would ever see me that way, hah, that would be a miracle; once upon a time, maybe, but not anymore. A girl can dream though, dreams full of sunshine, pools, staff to wait on your every need, a strong, trim, tanned and loving man at your side are free after all. Someone to laugh with, have fun with, someone to talk to without niggles and arguments, someone to care for you, care about you. Someone who loves you for who you are, enjoys you, sees you as desirable. That would be something worth working for, rather than enduring what I do simply to try and stay afloat. Perhaps I need a few more extra shifts so I can save up for a holiday, just ride the battles and demands for increasing amounts of money from Beau and be selfish for once. I know I can't though, for all her faults, she is lovely and I want to give her everything I possibly can so she can be happy; so if I do go on holiday, it would have to be with Beau.

    I would bloody well book somewhere more exotic than Broadstairs though. I laugh at the memory of last year's holiday. I can now, the distance of time helps make everything seem ok.

Broadstairs; I had dreamt of going back there, memories of my happy childhood holidays at the seaside had filled my mind and the place always seemed to want to draw me back, so it was something I desperately wanted to share with Beau. It didn't quite go to plan though if I am honest and I can now see it for what it was, a silly idea. I had had such high hopes for our holiday. I'd saved up for months, done extra jobs, worked longer hours, seen more patients, had even fewer treats. I had chatted endlessly to Beau about the lovely sandy beach where we could sunbathe, the sparkling sea we could play and swim in, the cute old fashioned streets we could explore, the pubs and cafes we'd be able to go to and really enjoy ourselves, go crazy, have fun, forget. Initially Beau really wasn't interested, as far as she was concerned, what was the point. If we were going on holiday, it should be abroad, somewhere exciting, not some dump of a seaside town on the South coast. I'd explained we would never be able to afford that, but this would be the next best thing, we would be able to get everything we dreamed off in little old Broadstairs and it would just about be affordable. Neither of us could remember the last holiday we'd had together and eventually she was as excited as I was. We booked a caravan just outside Broadstairs for a whole week at the end of June, went clothes shopping together, even got a new beach bag and some sunglasses. The holiday gave us a focus and we loved planning it and getting everything ready together, it was just what we needed to allow us to enjoy each other's company once again.

The big day came and we struggled on the tube to catch the train down to the coast; even that was exciting as we never usually get to go that far on the train together. I remember the train speeding off and us watching the city fall behind us as we travelled ever further into the open countryside, both pointing things out to each other, well, when there wasn't any phone signal Beau joined in. The caravan was lovely, a real home from home, more comfortable than our real home to be honest and it came complete with a picture postcard view of the sea. It was perfect; gulls screeching and squawking, the smell of salty seawater hanging in the breeze, the sunshine, kids playing and the ever present sound of laughter. That first evening we walked into town and had chips on the promenade overlooking the small sandy bay, chatting and looking forward to playing on the beach in the morning. Everything was good, we had made it and we were going to have a great week.

Hope is a wondrous feeling, lifting spirits and brightening moods, and I fell completely under its spell at the start of that holiday, forgetting in my naivety how it never lasts for ever and how callous it could be. That oversight made what was to come seem even worse; hope is certainly wondrous, but in the blink of an eye it can be left shattered, broken and empty when confronted with the cruel mistress of reality. Life is harsh and dreams easily shattered, and as I soon realised, that reality follows you even on holiday. Everything soon fell apart and all for an otherwise seemingly trivial reasons. Of course Beau wouldn't want to spend time with her mum, why should she? Wifi and phone signals mean everything when you live in a world where all your friends are connected in the cloud; so, it shouldn't have surprised me really that those two things would be the main consideration of where she would want to go and what mood she would be in. It became the norm that if she was connected, she would be in a good mood, but shut off from the physical world and totally absorbed in the virtual where her friends were; if not connected, and shut off from the virtual world, she would be in a bad mood and I would be held responsible. Either way, it wasn't much fun. It wasn't always like that though, every now and again there would be a momentary pause in life's emotional storm and I would fleetingly get my Beau back once again. On the rare occasion this happened, and it was these briefest of moments that I lived for, we would chat and joke and laugh and life would be brilliant again. She would giggle like the child she was when she splashed in the sea and forgot to manage the image she was so desperate to portray. She would marvel at the sights, the sun, the sea, the sunsets, the colours, when she actually looked up from her phone and noticed that was. She would suddenly become aware, take photos, enjoy being there, but never for long enough to make a difference. All too soon, she would be lost to me once again, totally absorbed in a conversation with someone who lived where we had just come from, catching up on meaningless gossip and living her normal life in the virtual world, not caring where she was, not needing to be anywhere in particular. It was heartbreaking to witness and undoubtedly my fault, she needs her friends far more than she needs me, she is and was transitioning from child to adult and getting more independent everyday. Like all teenagers, she wants to be treated like an adult, have adult things, eat adult meals, drink adult drinks, be an adult, most of the time. But then she will suddenly just be a child again, laughing at innocent things, always wanting sweets, crisps and puddings, but never, ever, for long enough these days. The tension between her desire to be online and absent from me, and my need to share the amazing place with her, made both of us frustrated and unhappy and we became increasingly distant from each other as the week went on, perhaps I should have booked only a few days. As ever, it was all my fault - I should know by now that you can never please everyone and if you can at least please yourself, that's better than no one at all.

It wasn't all bad though. We made up on the last day; she actually made the effort and chose to come and sit with me on the beach for a while and it was delightful as we just sat there enjoying the sights and each other's company as we shared a portion of chips. Suddenly, we were attacked by a flock of seagulls, swooping down and squawking as they pecked at our food, before flying away with their big wings flapping and our chips in their mouths. Beau jumped so much that the chips went everywhere, which encouraged even more gulls to join in for the chance of a quick meal, like a scene from Hitckock's 'The Birds'. Beau was hysterical and we both ran away screaming, but then fell on the warm sand laughing. Really laughing until our sides hurt. That moment was a keeper, a precious memory that I will always cherish even in the darkest of times. I wonder if Beau remembers, I hope so? I am still not completely sure if the holiday was a mistake or not, we had more than our fair share of conflict and tedium, but also fun and laughter. Just like life I guess.

I am just lifting my numb hand off the handlebar to take another bite of the banana that will have to see me through the day, as I haven't got any money to get anything else now, when I see wide eyes staring at me from the road in front. My mind can't quite comprehend the significance of what I am seeing. The first thought that rushes through my head is that I have seen this cat somewhere else recently, but where? The second is what on earth is it doing in the road. The fourth is to think fuck, I'm going to crash. The third was also to think fuck. The fifth is that I can't pull the brake as I've got a bloody banana in my hand. The sixth is that I can't swerve, else I'll hit an oncoming car. Before the seventh arises, I can see my front wheel hitting the poor little cat that was as shocked and slow to react as me. I see it flying up and landing on the pavement while I go over the handlebars because I panicked and involuntarily pulled the front brake. I spin in the air and land on my side in the road, with a car screeching behind me and horns blaring seconds later. Moments after that, people are crouching down and asking if I am ok; I am, I think, but I'm not entirely sure. It all happened so fast and I am more stunned and embarrassed than anything. I am helped to my feet and lowered next to the fence to pull myself together whilst some good-natured man gets my bike. It makes me realise just how kind people really are, there is always someone who will help.

I sit there nursing my aching arm and cut hands, but because I feel mortified and utterly embarrassed I tell everyone I am fine when they enquire. The traffic soon starts to move again as I focus on the banana, which has been squashed beneath a wheel, thinking that that could have been me, but as it was, it was just my breakfast. People carry on walking and I become just a curiosity now for anyone passing; life returns to normal and, once again, I feel alone and worthless. I look for the poor cat, but can't see it. I hope it will be ok, that was quite a knock I gave it. I feel bad, I should have been concentrating rather than day dreaming and eating.

I get to my feet and look at my bike, my heart sinks even further when I see that the handlebars are skew-whiff. I won't be able to get to Mrs Merrifield's on time now and so I will only have an even shorter amount of time with her; I have to cut the visits shorter than the expected thirty minutes as it is so that I can get to the next appointment. A whole day of being rushed off my feet, feeling like a failure, moving from appointment to appointment, never having enough time to give the comfort and help that these people really need, always having an eye on the time to get to the next poor soul; twenty visits today alone. I start struggling with the handlebars to try and straighten them as I need to get going, there isn't even enough time to feel sorry for myself. I am on the conveyor belt of life and so I just have to keep moving. Luckily, a middle aged man stops and helps me to straighten the bars; my saviour. I thank him and set off at double speed to try and get things back on track. What a day, it is even shittier than even I could have expected now; I've upset my daughter, nearly killed a cat, and will let an old infirmed lady down who is relying on me to help her. I will spend the rest of the day rushing from home to home, helping where I can, but constantly feeling sad that I can't do more. Life can be cruel. Can be, or is?

Frank - Colours of Life

My little friend hasn't been for the last few days, which is a shame. I have been putting out the tuna as usual just in case, but then having to throw it away again by mid-afternoon else it would start stinking and attract rats. I wonder where the little chap is?

I am up and dressed early today, I have got a lot to do as it is such a special day for us. I want to do something nice for our wedding anniversary. It is our sixtieth today, our diamond anniversary; if only we had been able to spend all these years together, but it wasn't to be and she was taken from me far too early. I love Rowena so very much, so much it still hurts. I know I should have got over everything by now really, but I can't as the heartache never goes away, it is always there, but every now and again it sneaks up on you and claws away right at your soul, making the emptiness and loss very much real once again. I still remember our Golden anniversary, I had been a sprightly young thing of only seventy-five then. The day had started like any other, we all go through little phases and different routines throughout our lives, but are never really conscious of the instance at which our actually habits change as they do so ever so slowly. At the time, I had been a regular at the local bowls club for years; always good clean banter, a bit of exercise and a reason to get up and dressed. It was a good place with good friends and the odd social evening thrown in too. I had just finished a game with a visiting team and we were all rather pleased with ourselves as we had played well and won the match. I was just having a pint of ale, when it struck me, it was my anniversary and I had clean forgotten. I had felt dreadful as normally I was quite good with dates. Just as I was chuckling to myself and about to buy the chaps a quick one for the road, it had hit me with a force that took the wind out of me. It wasn't just any anniversary, it was our Golden anniversary; special, very important and definitely something to celebrate.

Someone asked me if I was ok as I was standing mid way to the bar just staring into space and they all laughed saying I was just being big headed and reliving my moment of glory from the match. I laughed it off, of course, but then made my excuses and hurriedly left. Outside, I could hardly breathe, couldn't think and couldn't focus, because I was suddenly overcome with emotion, grief, sadness and despair. I felt wretched, I had forgotten, which was unforgivable. I had to get away and didn't want anyone seeing me being a silly old fool with tears in my eyes. This wasn't something to share, this was personal, for no-one else other than me. In that split second, when I realised it was our fiftieth, I felt so alone, so old, so lost. My love, my Rowena, gone. What should have been a celebration of our life together became a cruel reminder of the years forced apart; of lives shattered, love cut short. My despair was deeper than it had been in years as I had been caught so off guard; it had hit me unannounced and, worst of all, I had no one I could talk to about it, or at least no-one that would really understand. So, I did what seemed right at the time, I caught up with my old friend Mr Jack Daniels. I got a bottle, twenty cigarettes, even though I hadn't smoked for years, and smoked and drank my anniversary away in misery while flicking through photo albums and listening to our favourite records. The next day, whilst hungover and feeling even more sorry for myself, I resolved to never forget an anniversary and made a commitment from that day until we are together again, to celebrate our life and love rather than despair at our loss. I have done this every year since that awful day now and it helps me cope. So, I always make an effort these days, during the day I get my hair cut, put on a suit, get our favourite wine, buy some flowers and set the table for two before cooking Rowena's favourite meal in the evening, putting her picture next to me, playing one of her favourite records and just sit there, eating away and happily reminiscing about the time we had together; after all, she may not be here next to me, but she has been in my heart enriching my life all those years and that is definitely worth celebrating!

It was a real struggle to get ready today, but, as ever these days, there is no real need to rush for anything anymore if I am honest. My hands and fingers are playing up again and it takes me a while to get going and remember what I am doing. My feet and legs also hurt quite a lot again, they just do that nowadays for no apparent reason, so it will have to be short slow steps today, just for a change rather than racing round. I walk through the park after having negotiated the road, the lights at the crossing change back to green well before I have crossed, which is something you never realise will happen to you when you're younger. It is a good job that people are so patient and just wait there to let the silly old fool dawdle across. It is a nice park, full of life, colours and nature. It makes me feel alive and connected to the present moment when I am here, there is a slower pace to life and I don't feel as left behind as I do in the wider world outside its confines. It can get lonely by yourself sometimes, so it is nice to be with people and share something, even if that something is just the simple fact that we are all in the same park doing something — together, but not together.

I walk past a group of scaly wags skiving school, but they leave me alone, I am not a threat nor a target, I am just an old man walking slowly by, unnoticed, insignificant, inconsequential.

I get to Joe's and get the usual cheery 'Hello young man' from Joe as I enter, a chirpy Irish chap who is getting on a bit himself, although he must still be at least twenty years my junior. It is funny how when you are young, a year makes such a big difference and older kids keep themselves separate and distant from the younger ones, just in case they loose some of their mature coolness through association. When you are old though, it doesn't even become a consideration and people don't really see the difference between a sixty-something or eighty-five year old; when you have got white hair and wrinkles, age becomes irrelevant, you are just all old together.

Once it is my turn, I shuffle into the barber's chair and lower myself with a sigh - I smile as I remember Rowena telling me that you shouldn't act yourself into old age by sighing and such; she would still berate me even now, but I must admit I find comfort from my little sighs and shuffles these days if I am honest, they're just part of me. I go through the usual routine of pleasantries with Joe, same small talk he has got off to a tee and practiced like a pro on all his customers every time they come — it settles folks down I guess. I am sure he has a set pattern, trying to steer the discussions a bit, but always the same selection of subjects. He is cheery enough, always smiling and whispering conspiratorially in my ear, making me feel special, or that is his intention anyway. His eyes give him away though, the smile doesn't reach them as they are always looking at the door to see who comes in, assessing how long it will take to get through everyone before he can have a break, wondering how much money he will make and who will be a good tipper. I can't blame him, he does well to keep the facade going.

I look down at the cape covering my body, tucked in at the back of my neck with kitchen towel. It is funny how they have never found a more modern solution to prevent you getting covered in hair shavings. Some things are continually changing and developing, always being made better, faster, shinier and lighter; other things just seems to be ageless and are always just so. The barber's cape is one of them and I look down at my white hair clippings which contrast sharply with the dark material. I loose track of Joe's current story, it doesn't matter though as long as I just nod and grunt every now and again, he won't notice. Hair is a funny thing really, it changes continuously, yet we never really notice; always growing and changing colour like unnoticed markers of our lives.

Blonde. I remember when I was a young boy, I used to have almost the same coloured hair as I do now as it was so blonde. A right little blonde bombshell I was, just like my lovely Dad had been when he was a little boy too. A blonde 5 year old, full of life and fun, sitting in our kitchen with a sheet round my shoulders and my Mum chopping my hair in a bowl-like cut; big clumps of wavy blonde hair falling in my lap as it was unruly and just kept growing thicker and thicker, a never ending battle of wills to try and tame it for my poor old Mum. I would constantly be told off to sit still as all I wanted to do was rush outside and continue playing in the street with older kids on a little go kart my Dad made for me out of planks and old pram wheels. The road was obviously quieter in those days, hardly a car or bus in sight, we were more likely to see a horse than anything else; good roads for adventurous karters like us though who loved the thrill of speed. Always screaming to go faster and faster as the older boys pushed us down the road. I am sure they did it all rather begrudgingly, but it was my kart, so Charlie and I always had the first go and the older kids seemed to accept this and humour us. It was amazing, we would sit on the kart and feel our stomachs jump as we lurched forward, the speed increasing, the air rushing through my blonde hair and over my exposed legs. Charlie holding tight, me at the front as the older boys eventually let go because they couldn't keep up. The challenge was to see how far we could go until the others caught up again. We were just the right weight and size, so we whizzed along, straight and true, faster and faster, usually with our dog, Kip, happily bounding alongside all excited. The only fear was if the kart ever started to get a speed wobble as that could lead to it turning over and us being thrown onto the rough unforgiving surface. If that happened, our laughter soon turned to tears with the older boys then laughing when they finally caught up, took the kart and pushed it back up the hill for their go. All or nothing, that was what Charlie and my motto was; our tears never lasted long, no one got sympathy in those days, life was for living and having fun, not feeling sorry for yourself and certainly not for worrying about simple consequences such as hurting yourselves. Anyway, Kip would just come over, a somewhat knowing sympathetic look on his face, lick me and then start barking and getting excited again; no time to stay still. Life was fun and the horrors to come were unknown to us, we never knew the changes that the War would soon bring to our happy lives. You never really know what is going on in the wider world when you are a kid, you may sense something from your parents, but it never really penetrates your consciousness. However, it was to be less than three years later when we were all unexpectedly put on a train and sent into the countryside without our parents. I never saw Charlie again, his parents decided he should stay in the city and not be evacuated as they thought it would be safe enough; it turned out they were wrong, and I remember looking at the bombed out derelict house that had been Charlie's home when I returned from my holiday in the countryside years laters.

    Ginger, I had forgotten I was ginger. My hair went that colour in my teenage years, but it never really bothered me. During the War, we all grew up very fast — physically tougher and mentally more robust than we had been and able take to adversity, change and challenge in our stride; character building. My Mother was cutting my hair in the garden, it was always short now, so it wasn't clumps that fell in my lap, but small trimmings. My mother had decided, insisted, that I be as smart as I could for the Victory Celebration and parade. My anguish at the war finishing before I could serve was offset by the jubilant mood of everyone around me and it was impossible to not get caught up in the excitement of it all; we had won and the hardships were over, at last. The celebration was spectacular. We had a great spot on The Mall, we had got there early, and the atmosphere was electric. Obviously no-one noticed my new haircut, but that is just what Mum's do; fuss. We stood there mesmerised as four miles of mechanised army vehicles endlessly rumbled by, shaking the ground with their power. The firepower on display was amazing and something I would never forget, just what a 15 year old loved to see. The massed marching troops, with so many flags at the start and the different uniforms, sent everyone crazy; everyone loved the Greeks and I remember them getting a special cheer. After the troops, the air was darkened as hundreds and hundreds of planes flew overhead, but not like the bad days; these were ours, and everyone cheered, looking into the sky with straining necks. The celebrations and fun continued well into the night with a beautiful fireworks display, this was a real celebration and everyone was caught up in the moment, relaxing and loving life. You realise at times like this how precious life is and how much you miss friends like Charlie. Everyone had lost someone, but we were celebrating victory and that we had survived; life was going to be fun again and anything and everything was now possible. My life changed that night, Betsy became my first proper girlfriend, or I should say, Betsy became my first lover, in a very informal, but really rather fun way. I had started the War as a boy, but when it finished, I was well on my way to adulthood. I was happy, even if the victory had perhaps robbed me of my chance of personal glory.

Brown marked the next stage and my life had changed beyond recognition from the ginger teenage lad who had lost his virginity during the night of celebrations when the city went crazy. I can see my long brown hair falling in my lap; this time I am not at home nor in the yard with my Mother cutting my hair. Instead, I am in a rather well to do salon with a ridiculously expensive stylist cutting it. I am doing really rather well for myself at twenty-five, even if I do say so myself. Gone is the gloom of London, the austerity of the post war period, this is the mid fifties in Monaco and I am having my hair styled in a nice little place that gives me an espresso while I wait. The sun is shining and it is another beautifully hot and colourful day. After I have finished being groomed, I go outside into the glare of the sun and walk a short distance along the promenade to have another espresso, indulgence being the name of the game these days after all the rationing of my youth. I pick a table outside and spend a few minutes looking over the open expanse of the deep blue sea in the harbour where the yachts of the rich and famous are moored. One day I will have one of those, but it will not bring me the happiness I expect. As I sip the smooth and strong coffee, smoking the obligatory cigarette, I feel excited. I met a really rather delightful young lady a few weeks ago and things are going well. A real beauty, we met at a lunch party held by a mutual friend from the tennis club and hit it off straight away. Sometimes life just falls into place and you meet someone and things just click. It was as though we were having lunch by ourselves, I was absolutely mesmerised by her; beautiful smooth olive skin, lovely brown hair, funny, interesting, interested. Lunch flew by. Aah, Rowena had come into my life.

"Not disturbing you am I? I do love spending time with handsome men and I just saw you sat here all alone and couldn't help but pop over to try my luck! Are you expecting someone or can I intrude" I heard from someone next to me. Looking up, there she was and I couldn't help but smile. "Hello my love" I replied jumping to my feet, kissing her cheeks and embracing her. She was a sight to behold and I was rewarded with one of her wonderful smiles, a smile that made me feel I was special; I was certainly lucky. Dressed in a light turquoise blue two piece suit, the pleated skirt showing off her breathtaking legs — smooth, tanned, toned and alluringly exposed to just above the knee. Refined, classy, fashionable and showing off her figure just enough to still be modest; perfect.

She placed her ever present shiny black baguette style handbag on the table, sat down and ordered a coffee. Life couldn't get any better than that moment, sat in the sun, relaxing, chatting and being happy with the person I knew was my soul mate; I adored her and the expectation of our life to come was intoxicating. Rowena, even the name was special to me. Many a happy day we spent together, lunches, dinners, playing tennis, going out with friends, sailing, everything. Our love grew stronger every day and we enjoyed each other in every way that only true lovers can. Being with someone you love with all your heart, and who you think you can't love any more, but do, each and every day, became my life. And what an amazing life we had; glitzy, glamorous, party filled and always together with a joint, unifying and fulfilling love. I never wanted, or needed, to be apart, every moment was precious and I couldn't get enough of her, I remember feeling the need to maximise every second we had together. Despite feeling we had eternity before us, there was never a moment to lose by myself, our love was too special to waste. We married in sunshine that matched our moods and happiness; the world seemed to rejoice with us and it was the most amazing day of my life. We never wanted children, that was always in the future, the eternal, joyful, blessed future we would have together.

Salt and pepper, marking a turning point in my life, a time of change and sadness. Sitting on the deck of my yacht with long unkempt facial and head hair falling in front of me from my own hand. No pleasure in the simple cut, no event the reason, simply a necessity to prevent it becoming too long and unmanageable. No reason to care about the style, gone are my days of caring. I am forty, a lost soul, alone. How naive and presumptuous we had been about our plans for a never ending future of happiness. Denied to us is the chance to grow old and disgraceful together, our love torn away from us in the cruellest of ways. Rowena lost to me due to the curse of cancer. I have never known such sadness, never believed sorrow could physically hurt, that my heart could break. Hurt it did and hurt it does, every single day. As once my heart was filled with more love for her each and every day until I thought it could burst, now it fills with sorrow that never ceases and I feel it could implode; I wish it would. Our beautiful life came crashing down one sunny day after a visit to the specialist when Rowena had been feeling unwell. Our lives changed with a suddenness I had never expected nor known possible. Three weeks later, I was sat by her bed as she slowly slipped away, there was nothing I could do for the love of my life, I couldn't give her back the future she deserved, ease her pain or take away her suffering; all I could do was be there and try to provide her with some dignity, all the time having the feeling of being helpless, afraid and totally, and utterly, distraught. We had never had our children, life had been fun and there was always tomorrow. In the blink of an eye, there was no tomorrow and I was truly alone, by myself, without my Rowena. I had been in a daze from the moment I had said a final goodbye and sat through her funeral until I found myself sat one day in the middle of the street just crying my heart out. My sorrow flooded out of me and passers by avoided me, not knowing what to do or how to help. I couldn't understand the loss, couldn't find solace from the pain, couldn't find the will to live. I had given up my job and wallowed in our apartment, drinking and crying was all I could do, all the time surrounded by her things, our things. Eventually, I gave most of her clothes to charity, save a few with special memories, put all our possessions into storage, bought a small yacht, and sailed out of Monaco, never to return.

This was no trip of a lifetime, setting sail for some dream-like destination, this was escape, pure and simple. The yacht became my own island retreat, or rather my prison, somewhere to wallow, somewhere to be with my memories, somewhere to exist, nothing more. Storms fitted my mood, the solitude suited my sorrow. I just existed, always on the move, with no destination in mind, forever travelling to just leave my heart and dreams further behind; surviving the only way I could without my Rowena.

Wait for me my love, not long now.

Grey; not my mind set, my hair, I am old now, or I think I am, but I'm only sixty. You always think you are getting old, or are old, when you pass middle age, but you have years ahead still, if you are lucky, and healthy. I wear my hair short, it is starting to thin quite a bit and recede at the front, and I am having it cut at a nice little city barbers; Joe's. Having lost my way for years, I have finally sorted my life out and started to live again. The hole left in my heart from the loss of my Rowena is still there, and I still grieve, but the pain is not constant or all encompassing anymore. I realised that she wouldn't want me to waste my life and be a hollow shell just waiting for the end of my days. No, she would want me to live, to move on, to enjoy good times once again. Having sailed round most of the world, seeking solace in the expanse of the oceans and in the bottom of a bottle, I suddenly found myself arriving on the South Coast one overcast autumnal day a couple of years ago. It was as though I had woken up, I must have been conscious beforehand, but it was as though I had been in a daze, a daydream, and just come to my senses. Perhaps Rowena had finally got fed up with my behaviour and steered me home, who knows? I came to my senses, collected my things, mainly the photos I had taken during my travels, sold the boat and moved to the city of my childhood. Reminiscing over old times, happy days and forgotten memories, it felt good to be home, although times had changed much. Gone was the post war austerity and hardships, but so too were the boom years. Life was good, but the country was in a recession, although things were still much better than when I had last lived here. Bad news for many, but timely for me as I was able to buy a small little place in a nice part of town, on a very quiet road with a little park opposite. I knew Rowena would have loved it and the fact that I could afford the place after the wasted years gave me further thought that she had had a guiding hand in bringing me home at this time. She would have loved the cosy rooms, the quietness, the proximity to shops, the garden and the tree that we could put a bench under and sit together enjoying the sun. I still haven't got over the loss, but I can get on with life. I have gone back into business, sold the pictures of my travels and some of the ones I took, unseen until now, of poor Grace. I managed to get a job advising on a few new glossy magazines, including one focused on the lives of the rich and famous and one about travel. From a professional perspective, I love it, I am doing what I enjoy, travelling, and I am asked my opinion; I hadn't realised my reputation was so strong that it could have lasted so many years intact. Obviously I had known at the time that my pictures had been seen and admired by millions, but had never realised nor considered that my name was known so widely, in certain circles, and would be remembered. My life moves on and it is as good as it can get, but it will never be what it could, indeed should, have been. I have even been on a few dates with some ladies I met through work, and enjoyed intimacy on occasion, but nothing like what I had before. Life changed me during the dark years of my travels and the new start takes some time getting used to, but at least I want to live now. Friends, work, a home, a profession; not too bad, considering.

White. Now I am old, it is not until you reach the twilight years of your life that you realise you had never been old before. The aches and pains that start in middle age, the lines that start to appear on your once smooth skin and get deeper and deeper as time goes on, the hair that starts to thin and recede, all seem significant when you first notice them. But, when you are old, you realise the earlier signs meant nothing. After twenty-five years of coming to Joe's, my hair is thin and pure white as it falls from my head. I come here for the company more than anything most times, as well as from necessity and special occasions. My life has slowed down now and I could kick myself for wasting so many years when I was caught in the wilderness of despair. You get to a certain age and then you don't get old in the linear way you previously had; no, you get older exponentially and there is nothing you can do to stop it. You can fight it and struggle if you want. You can even try to hide it and pretend it is not happening, but you can't kid a kidder as they say, and age is the biggest kidder of them all. I enjoyed working at the magazines, but less than ten years later, it all got a bit much and I finally stopped. It wasn't just the fact that the travelling took it out of me, it was that my eyesight was not what it was and the cameras got increasingly more technical. It wasn't just that I didn't really understand all the different programmes and settings on the cameras, although that didn't help, it was that I had simply lost the knack and eye for a great photograph. Oh, I could still take good photos, but not great ones and I knew that was something I couldn't do anything about. I didn't so much run away, I just took a back step as time went on until I stopped completely. I had planned the transition and made sure I had a life outside of work to keep me ticking over. I didn't have a wife, how could I, and had never had children, so I made sure I socialised and had a circle of friends at the local pub, the bowls club and the amateur photography club. Life slowed down, but I was happy enough. It is funny though how when you first join something like a bowls club, you feel old, but are seen as one of the youngsters by the others; it was the first time in many years I had been called young and it made me smile. Then, as time goes by, life takes its natural toll and you soon become one of the elders, and then you see other youngsters joining, and chuckle about it if you remember. Seeing friends slowly take turns to take the final bow and join the afterlife becomes an almost everyday event. You become an expert at attending funerals and wakes, of saying goodbyes and of reminiscing; eventually, you become one of the few remaining souls left behind and that is when real loneliness sets in. Reminiscing is all you can do, life has been lived and you are just an old man who has been left behind; waiting your turn.

"There you go Frank, spick and span for the celebration eh! A handsome young devil once again!" says a cheery Joe.

I am brought back to the here and now with a jolt, I have obviously been lost in my thoughts again, it happens more and more these days; at least I didn't fall asleep this time though. I can see Joe has taken the cape off and is holding the mirror behind me so I can see the back of my head. It is funny really and makes me smile every time I come here, in the bright unforgiving light of the barbers I am looking at an old man who is looking at me. I see what others see and realise why they look at me the way they do, I just forget sometimes. I had better get up and pay, cheery Joe is eyeing me with a slightly less intense smile as he wants to get on to the next customer. I don't blame him, you have got to make hay while the sun shines after all.

I pay up and head back home through the park with that ever present feeling that I have forgotten something, but can't quite remember what. I am sure it can wait.

A New Beginning

I know I am lucky in so many ways. I had a near miss and a lucky escape, I am lucky not to have been more seriously injured, lucky to have been helped home, lucky to have been looked after, lucky to have people to care for me. Even Wilma hasn't been round in the night to scare me and crap in our plant pot. It hasn't been all good though I must confess; the V.E.T.S, as the people I share this flat with like to pronounce the word vets for some reason, may have meant well, but it is not nice having fur shaved off, being injected and having your temperature taken in a very unsophisticated, unpleasant and frankly invasive manner. Still, the man and woman who look after me have become far more tolerable since the accident by fussing, caring, being more considerate, giving me tastier food than before and even getting me a new comfier bed, although I do still prefer the sofa and have no idea why they think they can choose where I will sleep. I haven't been myself the last week or so and have not even been outside as a result. I have been spending my time focusing on recovering, getting stronger each day and feeling quite... loved. I haven't even minded having my fur rubbed as much as I did as I know they mean well, I can see the concern in their eyes and hear it in their voices. It turns out that they are pretty good people after all. They looked out for me, helped me and cared for me. It has been like having my own personal staff to look after my each and every need, which is rather nice; they are probably just feeling a bit guilty because they realise how annoying and lazy they were before. I could have started going out the other day, but I felt they were enjoying looking after me so much that I may as well let them indulge themselves for a while longer yet. I think today is the day though and I will go out to see how the world has been getting on without me.

It has been a weird few days, I have realised that the man and woman are actually quite nice after all and have surprised myself that I actually have feelings for them, other than absolute disgust and annoyance that is. I am not exactly sure why I never noticed before, or have they changed? Who is to say, but all I know is that it confused me and still does. I still have a desire to let him feel the paws and claws of power if he rubs my fur too much, but it takes longer than before until I really feel like giving him what for and he has usually stopped by then. Perhaps we all change and the accident affected us all one way or another. Perhaps I am even more tolerant and they are a bit more caring; perhaps they have always cared and I just never realised? Who knows? All I do know is that it is nice to feel that someone, anyone, cares about you — especially after having been so badly injured and feeling so alone and vulnerable. I feel happier and more at ease, more forgiving, more tolerant, more alive. It is an incredible but confusing set of emotions for me to feel, but I actually feel full of life and love.

They come into the room to check on me again and give me another stroke, it is nice, but does all make me feel a bit claustrophobic after a while. Whilst I don't mind them as much now, there are limits. The man kisses the lady, gives me yet another little stroke, watch it buddy there are boundaries still, and says, "I think our little puddy cat is getting better you know.

Anyway, I'd better be off or I'll never catch the tube. Loves ya." With that he tries to rush out of the door, but this is the moment I have been waiting for, he is at his most vulnerable now, in a rush and dressed in his dark suit, the perfect storm. He won't be expecting us to have our fun again as I haven't been in the mood for ages now. It is time to get back in the game though and show them I kind of like them, so I dash over to show some affection by rubbing my way all round his legs. "Surprise!" I squeal with delight "You're not a completely annoying arsehole after all and I'm feeling so much better, thanks for looking after me." All the time he is pirouetting like a ballerina trying to avoid me, but no chance; I am an expert at this tough-love malarky. Before he can do anything, his lower legs are covered in my hair and I feel rather pleased as I am feeling so much better and quite smug with myself. I got him, again! Our daily routine is back! He will never learn and I am rewarded for my efforts by the look of complete horror that crosses his face, only for it to be replaced with a smile. "Aww, welcome back little buddy," he says. He genuinely seems happy, although I am sure the glee will wear off in a minute when he tries to get all the hairs off before going out. I am happy too, I am almost back to normal and feeling much better.

The door is open, so I walk outside onto the terrace. Fresh air, mmmmm, I take a deep breath, filling my lungs and feeling the inflation lifting my ribs. I have never smelt anything so clean and pure as the fresh outside air; clearly it helps that Wilma hasn't been relieving herself in the pot recently. I can't remember enjoying the air quite so much before, feeling the breeze on my face and feeling happy, conscious of the sensations and simple pleasure of being outside. The man and lady come out and for a moment looking concerned and I am worried that they won't let me go, but then they smile, look at each other, hug and then kiss; yuk.

I am enjoying the freedom and decide it is finally time for a bit of exercise, so I go and perch on the top step to watch the world go by; after all, I don't want to wear myself out straight away, that would be crazy. I look at the road and watch the traffic, the bikes and the people. The poor, poor people. I look at their faces, see the sadness and realise that all they are doing is trying to get on with their lives as best they can under the constraints life has placed upon them. They are not all bad people, they just don't have a choice, they are just going to work and trying to get on with things, without making them any worse than they have to be, but forgetting they could make it better if they wanted too. I think about how no-one helped me when I was injured and how angry I was, but now I see that they probably just didn't notice; most of them are half asleep anyway. It is not that they ignored me deliberately, it is just that they weren't expecting something to be out of the ordinary and didn't see, all because they aren't used to looking.

With mixed emotions, I go back inside. I am confused, I really feel sorry for those poor people and can't understand why I never used to consider how they felt and that everything they seemed to do used to annoy me so much; weird. I lie on the sofa for a bit, not to have a little nap or anything so lazy, but rather to mull things over and have a little think about life. When I wake, I see that the lady person is sitting crossed legged again on a cushion in the middle of the floor. Eyes closed, she just sits there. I don't want to annoy her, for some reason I really don't anymore, but despite this, I still find myself being drawn towards her against my will as there is a certain energy and calmness that surrounds her when she does this, it is almost cat-magnet like. I feel myself being pulled towards her, ever so slowly but surely, by the tractor beam of calmness and find myself squeezing onto her lap before I can do anything about it. I think it is ok though as she doesn't seem to notice, although I am sure I saw an eye momentarily peep open. The stillness is all very comforting and we just sit there, together, contemplating and being present in the moment.

A while later, the traffic has calmed down slightly, so I nip outside to get closer to my public. I head straight down the stairs and sit on the wall, watching. As ever at this time of day, the sweet smell of cherry wafts over me and there is the ever present noise of laughter. Rather than resenting the interruption, I watch the young mum and her son. They do seem genuinely happy and the boy is really laughing, he is in his school uniform with a small rucksack over his shoulder. I am surprised that people make their young ones conform at such an early age, making them wear dull coloured clothes and follow such set routines, but it is presumably all to get them ready for when they have to grow up and live the lives expected of them; conforming, commuting, existing. It is sad really. At least the young lad next door is fighting it, he has some sort of red cape over his school clothes and pretends to fly around his mum. They are good together and lucky to have each other, anyone can see that from the broad smiles on their faces. The boy dashes inside, arm extended in front of his body as he runs in laughing. I continue to look at the mum; the smile narrows as soon as the boy has gone and I sense, then see, that it doesn't actually extend to her eyes and that it is partly for show. I have never really looked at people's eyes before, but I realise they can say a lot about a person, if you pay attention and observe rather than just watch.

Deep down, she is sad, I can see it clearly now, how could I have missed it, how could anyone not see it; how can anyone not try and help? As soon as her son comes back, the smile widens again and she is fixated on him once more, making him happy and laugh is all she seems to want to do, she is completely absorbed. As soon as he has gone, her eyes loose their focus and shine once more and a weariness seems to descend over her; perhaps it is all due to Wilma, but then even she doesn't seem too bad really. The lady is just sitting there, staring out at an unseeing world, unnoticed, unobserved, just puffing clouds of sweet cherry into the air. With a start, I realise I feel sorry for her, I can sense her sorrow and it makes me sad that I can't help; how can she be unhappy, why is she unhappy, and why doesn't anyone notice or even look at her? Whilst I am watching her, I see that she suddenly starts to focus on something, I follow her gaze and observe a well dressed man walking down the road in a posh suit, shiny shoes and a coffee in his hand. She is obviously trying not to catch his eye, but is interested, and as he passes I see him looking over at her out of the corner of his eye. She is not looking at him, but I am, and I notice his eyes sparkle when he sees her and a smile fleetingly warms his face that gives him a slight bounce in his step. He doesn't break his stride though and just walks on by, pretending not to notice her and thinking she hasn't noticed him either, but I saw the way he looked at her and the way she is clearly interested in him. She doesn't seem to look at him critically and it momentarily breaks her out of the default mode many people seem to have when they are focused inwards on themselves, it brings a certain life back to her. Her gaze follows him when he has passed and she watches him disappear down the street until her son comes back out and she switches her attention back to him instead; interesting.

They both stand and set off across the road through the park. I see the traffic is quiet and so I follow them into my haven. I haven't been here for a while now, not since the accident. I know I have a set patrol route, but feel like just taking it easy and doing something different. It is a beautiful sunny day and life seems too good to waste with simple routines, after all, I am not a robot. I realise I must have been as bad as everyone else, all those people just absorbed in functioning rather than living and I don't want to be like that any more. It is as though I have suddenly been given my consciousness and awareness back. I sit in the park and don't just see what is going on, I actually consciously observe what is going on, right here and now — not in the past or the future, but now. I sit for a while and bask in the feeling of my body being caressed by the sun's rays, smothering me in a blanket of warmth, enjoying the slight breeze on my face and the fresh air filling my lungs. The birds are singing, they are happy too; I wonder what is special about today, the world seems happier in the park than normal, full of life. Perhaps it has always been so? I walk for the sake of it, feeling the reassuring pressure of the contact of my paws on the soft grass, I am consciously being present and it is wonderful. I can feel my breath, I am actually aware of breathing! This is amazing; every cool intake of air giving me life, filling my lungs and energising my body, with each exhalation taking the slightly warm air from my body ready to be recharged by the next. I can smell the grass, the sweet smell of the recently cut grass contesting with the more earthly smell of the longer wild grasses. The park is no longer just a hunting ground, and never was really, it is a paradise, an oasis of calm in the hectic city, full of smells, aromas, sounds, life. It is breathtaking and I feel so very happy, my life feels fuller and richer than before; how could I have missed all this when I have been here before? It is incredible and I feel as though I have suddenly unleashed a super power, the power of consciousness.

A barking dog causes me to freeze, but when I look, all I see is a big black and white dog just having fun chasing a ball with its human. It is nice; they are not out to hurt anyone, they are just having fun, enjoying the moment and their companionship. I suddenly wish that everyone could experience the joys of the park, to come in and enjoy life rather than walking round the outside and never really coming in. So sad.

I spend a while longer in the park, not patrolling or hunting, just enjoying being here, consciously being here. Wow, I feel as though I am on sensory overload today and just wish everyone could open their hearts and experience this feeling too, even if only fleetingly.

After a while, I head back towards home and go via the little house with the tuna, but unfortunately there isn't any food available when I get there. I hop on the window sill and get a surprise, the old man is sat in a chair, in his pyjamas as ever, with a white bandage wrapped around his head and his arm is in a sling. I wonder what has happened to the old chap and hope he is ok, perhaps he has been in an accident like me. It certainly doesn't look like the sort of thing that would be good for someone his age. Our eyes meet and I am sure I see a slight smile appear on his face just before he looks like he starts to say something, his lips are moving, but I can't hear what it is. I watch for a while longer, but he doesn't move, he just sits in his chair and silently talks. I hop down and am just about to go, when I hear the front door being opened, which always puts me on alert. I am about to dash out of the garden, when I get my next shock of the day, and this one stops me in my tracks. Standing there, with a bowl of what I can smell as tuna, is the lady who ran me over! What on earth is going on here and I wonder if she ran the old man over too?

"Hey, hello little chap," says the lady, in a surprisingly friendly light tone. "Frank said you'd go hungry if I didn't give you this, he's been worried about you. Here you go."

She places the bowl on the floor and just watches me, before turning and shouting to the old man inside that I am here. I am sure she recognises me, but not fully, and there is certainly no malice in her eyes. She seems like a kind person, but like the mum, she has a sadness about her and seems rather preoccupied, like she wants to relax and be present, but can't for some reason, perhaps she has just got too much on her mind to break free. I walk over and have a little of the tuna, it is fresh and lovely. "He gets this specially for you every day," she says stroking my back, "but between you not coming for a few days and Frank having a fall and being out of action, he was worried about you."

She heads back in, but leaves the door open. "Frank love, the cat's loving the tuna and seems fine. I'll just sort your lunch out and bring it in for you to have later and then I'll pop back round this afternoon okay? I'll have to go soon as I've got another appointment to keep in St Mary's Square, but I can make you another cuppa if you want before I go?" Feeling unusually brave, because they seem such nice people, I decide to wander in as I find myself keen to see what the old man is like. I go into the front room, which is so unlike where I live, that is sparse and empty compared to this place, as there are things everywhere, mainly photos in frames and nicknacks. I like it immediately, it is cosy and has a pleasant aroma. The old man is in an armchair by a little fire that has been lit despite it being sunny outside, this is definitely my sort of place.

The old man sees me and gives me a little smile, he has got a kindly face, a face lined with stories and memories. Despite his seeming drowsiness, there is still a twinkle of life in his eye, now that is something you don't see every day and I certainly didn't expect to see it in someone so old.

"Hello little chap, I was hoping you would pop in sometime. Makes all the wasted tuna worthwhile, well, as long as you're not a tuna," he says with a raspy wheeze. There is just enough room on his lap and, as he doesn't look like a fidgiter, I gently hop up. He is warm and has a comfy lap that I snuggle in to. His first reaction isn't to try and dust off hairs like some people do, he just gently reaches over and rubs my ear; ooh, that is nice.

"Here you go love," says the lady placing a cup of tea and a biscuit on the little table next to him. "See you've made a friend there. Do you want me to put it out or do you want to leave him? I can always let him out later if needs be." The old man says she can leave me, which is no problem with me either, not that I was asked. He seems a good-natured, snuggly man who could do with a bit of company, so I will risk it and am happy to stay.

The lady gives me a quick stroke, says cheerio to the man and then I hear the door clicking shut as she leaves. It is just the old man, me, a nice warm fire, a clock ticking away on the side and the radio quietly playing some soothing tunes; lovely.

"She's a lovely one that Clare," he says, "I need a little bit of help after my fall. She's so kind, really wants to help, makes sure I'm okay and can't do enough for me. She doesn't even need to come back later, but she says it's no effort as she lives local. I bet it's the last thing she needs really, but I'm so grateful. There aren't many folks like that, that really care, these days."

We sit there, just enjoying each other's company. It is like we have been friends for years, sometimes it just clicks and you feel comfortable and relaxed with someone. He tells me how he fell over when he was trying to do a bit of gardening and hit his head on a bench and couldn't get up. Luckily someone was doing some work on the house behind, saw him and called an ambulance. "It was awful" the old man says, "I hate making a fuss and it was such a scene. I was so worried they'd keep me in hospital and then that would be that. You get to a certain age and it's best if you stay out of hospital and be independent in your own place. Luckily, they didn't have any beds and I wasn't too bad, so I managed to convince them I'd be okay. They agreed, but insisted on organising me some help for the next few weeks. I was worried it would be a matronly and fussy busy-body they would send who treated me like a child, but luckily, it was Clare. She couldn't do enough that one, she's a god send"

He certainly likes to talk, in between dozing; he seems to split his time between both, always with a reassuring hand on my back. I haven't felt quite so relaxed in ages. He tells me about his wife and I wonder where she is. I learn about his background, how he was a famous photographer and how one of his most famous pictures, which he points out on the sideboard, is of a princess, whatever that is, called Grace Kelly. He seems almost as smitten with her, in a friendly brotherly way, as with his wife, who it is clear he absolutely adores and dotes over. He has so much to say, but obviously seems to think he won't have enough time to get it all out, so needs to rush and be on constant send. Who would have thought an old person could be such a chatter box; poor old chap just needs some friends to chat to or some family. I wonder where they are.

The creaking of the door opening wakes me from a deep, restful sleep. I am a bit disorientated, but then realise I am still on the old man's lap; we have both been snoozing. I must have been here for hours, it feels strange to feel so relaxed and comfortable, yet so right. Clare walks in and starts chatting to the old man as he wakes up. I need to stretch my legs, so hop down and arch my back, which feels good, before going to the door as I need to relieve myself and think it best done outside. I look at the old man before I go, he seems content. I will be back I think.

Rather than going home, I feel like another stroll in the park. I have been cooped up for ages now and it is nice to be outside again. I dash over to the park, having checked for cars and bikes first, and decide to visit the far side to see what is going on over there. The first thing I notice is the fantastically vibrant colours of the flowers, which are beautiful, even in the dimming light of early evening, and smell divine. Yellows, oranges, whites, reds, even blue; every colour. Nature is wondrous and I can't quite believe this is the first time in my life I have really noticed it all. I could kick myself, but I am so glad I can see it all now in brilliant surround sound and glorious technicolour, with real smell-o-vision thrown in for added pleasure. I could just wander here forever, well, until it gets too dark and chilly to be more honest. In my almost dream like state of noticing everything, I almost miss the danger. I come out of the flower bed, and find myself confronted by a homeless guy, who is really quite filthy and rather smelly, sat on the ground with his meagre belongings next to him, an old dirty rucksack with a sleeping bag stuffed in a roll on top, and a carrier bag with a few bits in it. I am just about to run away, when I notice that although he has seen me, he is not really interested in me. He appears to be smiling and is looking towards the big houses; my first thought is he is a burglar casing the joint, getting ready to steal something or generally get up to mischief. But then I begin to doubt that as he is not concealed and isn't looking around to see if he has been spotted. He is just sat there, leaning against a tree, smiling.

I feel drawn to look at whatever has got his attention and move next to him, following his gaze. He puts a hand out and, rather than grabbing me or shooing me away, he gives me the gentlest of strokes, all the time just looking across the street.

"Now that is a wonderful sight my little friend," he says in a soft lilty voice, looking at me while he talks with a contented look on his face. I try to see what has caught his attention, but can't see anything other than a man and woman painting a front room, with a light on that is very bright and highlights both of them, in one of the houses across the road. I can't begin to identify what it is he has seen, it can't be that, those houses are huge, probably expensive, and here he is with all his belongings in a couple of smelly bags.

"That's adorable isn't it?" he says again, but not to me this time, almost to himself. "I bet they've just moved in, a whole lifetime of dreams and happiness ahead of them methinks. See that lady holding the little ladder? Well, that bump isn't because she's had a few too many choccie biscuits you know. She's got a bun in the oven, so there'll be the patter of little tiny feet in that house soon enough, you mark my words."

I really don't know what to make of this. Is the guy drunk? I can't smell that sweet musty aroma that those type of people usually have, and he isn't speaking weird or got glazed eyes. No, he hasn't been drinking alcohol. He just seems genuinely happy for those people. Weird, but why?

"Now, I'll never have what they've got, that's for sure, at least I won't have the money for a house like that you see. But I can only hope I get myself settled and find myself a lovely lady one of these days. That would be grand wouldn't it my friend? Rich people are allowed to be happy too aren't they now, and it's not the things that make them happy, and I'm sure youse know that my little friend. You see, happiness is just a state of mind, it's not about things. Possessions don't make anyone happy really, they're just the extra packaging of life, some people have things and some don't, and some people are rich whilst others will always be poor, that's just the way of things to be sure. But now, the secret of life, the thing that makes me feel happy even when I'm cold, hungry and could be feeling sorry for myself, is that we all have the ability to be positive, look on the bright side of things and have dreams. No one can stop you dreaming my friend, because everyone has a chance to find happiness and love don't they? That's the secret of life and what keeps me going; once you know that, what's there to be sad about now? Everything changes, so too will luck. And with luck, I'll be like those two fine folks over there; in love and happy. Sure it'll be somewhere they'd never give a second look at and would probably turn their noses up at, but it'll do me. A little somewhere with a lovely girl to share it with is all we can hope. And so they make me feel happy, really truly and utterly happy."

He has been stroking me the whole time he has been talking. Gently stroking me while he chats away in his melodic soft voice, watching the people decorate, with a smile on his face and, as I realise, a tear in his eye. Who would have thought it? Homeless people care, which is more than some who have more, and can be nice, happy, optimistic dreamers who just need a break with their luck. What a lovely and loving guy this is. He has nothing, but can be happy for folks with everything, and not be jealous of their possessions as doesn't want those anyway. He just wants what everyone can have, if they are lucky, and that is just to be in love with someone.

To love and be loved; priceless, but free.

We sit for a while longer, then he shakes his head, gets up, puts on his pack, picks up his bag, gives me a final stroke and then says, "May you be well and may you be happy my friend."

With a final look at the couple, he gives me a smile and heads off through the park.

'Be lucky my friend, be lucky' I shout after him, and I mean it.

Ellie - Heroine in the Park

Fucking hell, Ben is such a twat these days, I've no idea what planet he's on. He's really going off the rails and will end up locked up soon if he's not careful. Even Jake and the others seem to want to distance themselves from him now. It's one thing bunking off and not giving a shit about school, it wasn't even too bad when he just smoked weed and stole the odd bit from the shops, after all we've all done that, even getting into fights and trying to be the hard man; everyone could live with that. No, he's just gone mental now, as if nothing can stop him.

We're sat on the wall at the park chatting, there's a big group of us as it's Saturday and everyone has come to look at Ben's latest handy work. Some are excited and there's a bit of a buzz, but lots of us just think he's a knob, good and proper. The bollards blocking the path have been smashed over and there is a burnt out wreck of a car about a hundred meters into the park. A black hulk, with scorched grass around it and puddles where the fire brigade, who only just left, had to put it out in the night. The police are still here and have already been over to chat to us. Ben may be a twat, but no-one would snitch and he knows that. He's being the big 'I am' but we all saw he was shitting it when they came over.

"Yeah, fucking awesome it was" Ben says for the fiftieth time today already, "t'was easy as you like man, we just took the car from next to Stan's place and went for a spin. Mad it was, who knew driving on weed would be so much fun!"

"Yeah yeah," says Liam, "but you were shitting it when the Bill came over, I thought you'd faint and shit yourself there and then!"

We all laugh at that, which causes the nearest policeman to look over at us again and we all involuntarily go quiet. I actually feel guilty even though I've done nothing wrong.

"Fuck you Liam," Ben replies, trying to face up to him, "you know you'd never have the balls, all you'll do is homework for a buzz, live life in the fast lane eh? Twat."

"At least I'll get some qualifications and be able to fuck off out of this shit hole. You'll still be here drinking out of some bottle from your dole money for the rest of your life. Prick," is Liam's reply.

The group is fairly evenly split, those who seem to think Ben's some kind of hero, living the life they'd love to, being free and adventurous, and those of us that think he's a right looser. The group will split fully soon I'm sure, there's a tension simmering under the surface and everyone will start to go their own directions soon enough, after the exams, if not before. Liam has a point, we know it and Ben knows it. Not to be belittled and put down, Ben suddenly punches Liam on the side of his face, knocking him to the floor. The group reacts, not like the old days when everyone would gather round shouting 'fight, fight, fight' but rather the two sides face each other off and jostle the other.

"You're a fucking loon you twat," shouts Liam as he gets up

and touches his split lip, looking at the blood. "I'm getting out of here, who's coming?" he asks looking around for support; my friends all agree and we walk off to the taunts from the sados who stay behind, it'll probably all be on Snapchat before we're out of the park. Hopefully Ben will say something that links him to the car, he's a liability and needs locking up before he really gets out of control and hurts someone.

We go into town for a drink at the shopping arcade.

"Want a Starbucks El?" asks Hannah

"No thanks, I'm okay cheers" I respond. I'd love one, but my fucking mother is so tight with money and it's embarrassing to keep scrounging off everyone. It's so unfair, they all have money, I didn't even get a tenner. What a tight arse. 'Do you know what I have to do to get this' Mum screamed at me this morning; fucksakes, all I did was ask for some money for a frappe. Fuck, I hope I get a better job than being a dogsbody and skivvy for a living; she should have paid more attention at school.

"Here you go, I got you one anyway," Hannah says, "just in case you change your mind."

She's so sweet Hannah. I guess it's easy to be thoughtful when you have money. Her parents both work and she has a nice house on Fairfields, gets everything she wants, lucky cow. But then her parents never seem to want to do anything with her, they even go on holiday by themselves these days and won't take her, she never eats with them either and they hardly speak. At least she gets money though.

It's strange, but the more we talk about it, the more we both want the other's parents; she'd like a mum who always gives you the third degree and takes you on crappy holidays, I'd like a mum and a dad who give me stuff and get off my case. I'll be like both of them when I have my own kids; one day. When they all head off shopping, I make my excuses and head off home going through the park.

I'm nearly home, when I see a group of lads, Ben and some of his 'posse' pushing and jeering someone. It's more noise than anything, but as I get nearer, I see it's an old man with a bandage round his head, he looks dazed, confused and very scared.

"Fucking dirty old pedo" one of the gang is shouting, "what ya doin in the rec, come for a crafty wank over the kids in the park eh".

"Disgusting old cunt!" shouts Ben jabbing his finger in the old man's chest so hard that he staggers back.

"Oi, fucking leave him alone you twats," I scream running over. I'm not sure why I'm so angry, but this is going way too far now. I can see the poor old man is terrified and it angers me how they're treating him. I get my phone out, take a picture and shout.

"If you don't fuck off, I'll call the police, tell them you're mugging this poor sod and tell them it was you that fired the car!"

"You wouldn't fucking dare. Fuck off," he shouts back.

"Okay," I scream back "fucking watch me."

I start dialling and he runs over, pushing me, spittle flying in my face as he starts pushing me and shouting.

"You're a fucking twat Ben, leave the old man alone and fuck off. I will you know, I'll tell them it's you".

I can see he's furious, off his head, but he's also unsure.

"You're a fucking bitch you fucking slag," he shouts, "You'll be fucking sorry, you fucking watch out".

"Come on" he shouts to the others, "let's leave the old twat with slut-face here". They then move off and I watch them go, calm as you like as if it was nothing to them and the old man has been forgotten; wrong place, wrong time. The old man is just standing there shaking.

"Hey, it's okay," I say, "they've gone. Are you all right? Do you live round here?"

He's dazed and doesn't reply at first, finally he stares at me, well through me at first. I put my arm round him and the poor thing flinches at first, but then seems to see me for the first time.

"Have they gone? What did they want?" he asks "I haven't got any money, I only came here to get some fresh air. Will they come back?"

"No, they've gone. You're ok. Let's get you home, where do you live?"

He points to the main road and we slowly walk together towards the gate. I feel protective of him and want to see him home safe, just in case Ben comes back. It seems to take an age as he's so slow and keeps looking over his shoulder, but finally we get to his little house. Quite a nice place actually. I have a final look around to make sure Ben's not watching, and then he goes in and invites me to follow.

It's a bit smelly and cluttered, but homely. I like it.

"Thank you my dear, you're very kind," he says once we're inside and I've helped him shuffle to his chair. "I have no idea what they were after or what they would have done if you hadn't helped me. Why me, I have never seen them before? I have been going in that park for twenty-five years now and never been attacked. Thank you."

"Hey, no need to thank me. They're just idiots always looking for trouble, it wasn't you they were after, they were just looking for anyone because they're in a bad mood," I reply. It was true what I said, but how senseless is it all; poor old man.

"I'm El, Ellie, by the way. Would you like a cup of tea, Mister?"

"Frank, my name's Frank my dear. Yes, please."

I make him a cup of tea, there's not much in the fridge or any of the cupboards. I take it in and sit by him. "Are you not having one?" he asks. "No thanks Frank, I'll be off soon. Will you be okay?"

He says he will be fine. He's got a helper, a nice lady who comes in morning and night to help him with a few bits since his accident. He can't speak more highly of her, she sounds lovely and even comes when she's not being paid. At least there are some nice people in the world.

I'm just about to say my goodbyes, when I change my mind. I feel sorry for him, so I say I'll have a cup of tea and go to make myself one. When I come back in, he seems more settled and we chat. He stops worrying about Ben, the twat, and asks me to put on a record as it soothes him. He wants the soundtrack to Breakfast at Tiffany's as that's his favourite, apparently his wife loved it too. I find the record and take it out the beautiful old sleeve, unsure what to do with it as I've never used a record player before, they're so old fashioned. He laughs, tells me there's nothing that can compare to vinyl and instructs me how to put it on the player, switch it on and put the needle on. A moment after lowering the arm, the soft crackly music starts, it sounds amazing and I have to agree it's soothing. We sit and chat for a while before I notice he has lots of photographs around the room.

"I love photographs" he says, "it's always been my passion. I've still got a camera somewhere and keep meaning to get it out so I can take a picture of the little cat that comes round. He comes round every day now to sit on my lap, and eat my tuna, you need to give cat's something for their attention you see. A gorgeous little thing, lovely company. It's a new camera, one of those digital ones. I can't get the photos off it, but I can just about see them in the viewfinder. Still like to keep my hand in."

I explain that I want to be a photographer and always take pictures wherever I am. I sit on the arm of his chair and show him the ones on my phone, zooming in so he can see the detail. "They're very good," he says. I look at him, the old flatterer. "No, I mean it, you've got a good eye. You should stick with it, with a bit of luck you can make a go of it. Everyone thinks it's a dying art these days because everyone can take pictures. The difference is that a *photographer* takes a memory and captures the right moment. Other people just take a picture. You need the eye to see a good scene, to capture it just right. You're good. What camera have you got?" I tell him that I haven't got a camera as my tight arsed mum won't buy one for me. He looks horrified for a moment and then laughs, I tell him I love her really, but she's just a bit tight.

I ask about some of the pictures he has out. There are lots of his wife, who was taken before her time he says. The others are from his different jobs and trips. He's especially proud of a lady, Grace Kelly he says, who was a princess in Monaco and he was her personal photographer for a while, including her wedding.

"I'm sure you've never heard of her, but she was a real super star of her day," he says. "Everyone loved her, she was an actress, pretty as a picture and a lovely genuine person toboot who then became a real princess. They were such happy days and she never had a bad photograph in her, very photogenic she was, made my life easy really."

We spend a while longer talking about Grace, her life, Monaco, the amazing party she held for the birth of her son, with free champagne for everyone apparently. I can only wonder at things like that. "I've got albums of photos from that time," he says. "You'll have to come and have a look at them. Sorry, only if you're interested, I wouldn't want to bore you."

"No way!" I say, "I'd love to, thank you. I've never met a real photographer before, and now I've met someone who's photographed royalty! I'd love to, honestly. Can you teach me some photography skills as well, I'm doing it at school, but the teacher's rubbish?"

He says he will and I can come round any time, but not too early as it takes him a while to get going in the mornings. I like Frank and ask if he wants me to bring anything round when I next come. His reply, after firstly saying no, is that it would be good if I can get him some tuna for the cat, and he gives me some money; he's so trusting.

I leave feeling happier than in a long time. I've met someone who did what I want to do and he has had an amazing life, it makes my dreams seem more real somehow. Who'd have thought it? I end up going back to see him most days to chat as it's the holidays and everyone else seems to be a bit distant now after the falling out; time changes, relationships change and life moves on. My visits are fascinating and I'm learning more than I ever thought possible. He always asks about me and what I think, but I haven't really got much to say as I realise I haven't really experienced life, but he certainly has. I can't imagine the life he's had and only hope I can do a fraction of what he's done. He talks about his carer, but I haven't seen her; she sounds lovely though. It's fun spending time with him and I never thought I'd say that about an old man. I love the photos, the albums, the records, the stories, the lessons and even the temperamental cat that eats all the tuna.

In such a short time, he's done more for my future than the teachers or my mum ever have, he's sort of the grandad I've never known but wish I had. One day I'll make it. One day.

Goodbyes and Tears

I can't believe she got me again, scared the life out of me and nearly finished me off this time she did. At least she was good enough to let me recover for a while, but she just can't help herself I guess. There I was, in the sun again, gloriously warm and sat on some luxuriously soft silky cushions, when I was rudely dragged back to reality, kicking and screaming, into a nighttime nightmare with a beast stalking me. She gets me every single time, it must be too tempting for her to stop. It would be funny, well, it is funny I guess, apart from I think my heart is going to physically explode and I will die from a heart attack one of these days. Same routine as ever, although after a break of a few weeks, it seemed even more nightmarish. I will have to think of something to get her back, perhaps I will stay out one night and give her a surprise — she wouldn't be expecting that and with luck I might be able to give her so much of a fright she won't dare come back as she will discover who really rules this roost. I will have to have a good think about it, as whilst the thought of getting her back is appealing, the thought of being outside, in the dark, sends involuntary shivers down my spine.

Anyway, another glorious day ahead. Yummy biscuits, a stroll in the lovely park, followed by tuna and cuddles at the old man's before an evening relaxing at home. Heaven! Life is so much more enjoyable when you don't fight it but rather just look for the positives.

After another productive morning filled with food, ablutions, rubbing hairs on the man's suit as he heads out, just because I can, and sitting with, or rather on, the cross legged woman whilst her eyes were closed when sat on a cushion cross legged, I head out. Another beautiful day to be alive, and boy, do I enjoy life these days — to the full!

The young mum is there, as ever, puffing clouds of sweet smelling cherry vapour into the air, on the steps of her house, laughing with her little boy. Same routine, same seeming happiness, but the omnipresent same slight sadness in her eyes whenever alone. Poor thing, I wonder what is on her mind and why she's not truly happy? I catch her looking at the young suited man as he walks down the road again, it is funny now that I am aware of it, seeing their daily ritual of how they both look at each other, but don't want to be seen doing so and don't see the other looking at them. Such a waste really, why people can't just be open and honest and talk to each other I have no idea. They clearly want to talk, but just can't bring themselves to make the first move for some bizarre reason. Silly, I now know that life is way too short and precious to waste any opportunities. Still, there is always tomorrow I guess?

The park is as wonderful as ever; colourful, peaceful, full of wildlife, with fluffy squirrels hopping across the grass like stones skimming across a pond, birds full of song, making nests and preparing for their new offspring, flowers in bloom and trees in blossom. Chock-a-block full of life and vibrancy. The air is warm and still, the sun is shining, dogs are walking people and making them pick up their poo, which still amazes me, and joggers are out in force. Life always seems better when the sun is out, things look better and people seem happier.

I do the rounds, but more to experience the smells and sights of the park these days rather than anything else; no sign of Wilma, which isn't expected at this time of day, but is good nonetheless! Once done, I wander over to the old man's house, he always seems pleased to see me and I have got the timing just right now, so that the lady who pops in to help him is there to let me in, after I have eaten the tuna of course. It is a nice little routine we have going here now. I get to the house, with its overgrown but natural looking garden that makes the statement that nothing is false or forced here. The bowl of fresh tuna is out and so I help myself, it would be rude not to.

"Here he is," says the lady as she opens the door to the man who is, as always, sat in his chair in the homely little room he likes so much.

"Are you sure you don't need anything Frank?" she asks the old man.

"No thanks Clare my dear, you do more than enough. I get a little help from that nice girl who comes round, the one who helped me when I was set upon by that horrible bunch of young lads. She's such a lovely girl, really thoughtful and kind. She gets the tuna and a few bits for me and pops round later in the day. She's a good listener you know, loves her music and has a real eye for photography, she will make a real name for herself when she's older. She's a natural, she has a real passion and intuitive talent and the determination to make a career of it. Can't be many kids her age like that you know."

"I wish my Beau was like that. Right little madame she is, I'm so worried about her Frank, I just don't want her to end up like me. Running after my shadow all day, struggling to make ends meet, no chance of a holiday. Same old same old, eh? Still, could be worse. At least I go to work and get back in the light this time of year, I do love the spring and summer."

"Hopefully it'll work out for her," he responds. "It has got to be difficult for youngsters these days. It always was a hard time in anyone's life. Almost an adult, but still a kid, wanting independence but still needing their parents for everything, sick of school and education but not knowing what they really want out of life. Yes, it's hard for them. I'm sure you're a good Mum and hopefully things will work out for her."

"Yeah, she's not all bad. Anyway love, I'd better get going, no rest for the wicked. I'll pop back later dear. Enjoy the day with your little friend."

"You're far from wicked and you work too hard. Honestly, there's no need for you to keep coming round and putting yourself out on my account," he responds. But Clare doesn't really hear as she is in full motion now, a whirlwind finishing off and preparing to go.

"See you later," she says as she heads out of the door. When she has gone, the house seems so quiet, just the ticking of the clock and the faint noise of the outside world coming through the closed windows. The fire is lit, which is always welcome. You have got to love old people if they are all like this; quiet, relaxed, friendly and always chilly enough to need a good fire.

"She's lovely that Clare," he says looking at me from his chair, "so thoughtful. She even moved my record player and some albums so I can reach it from the chair because she knows I love listening to my memories crackling away to break the quiet loneliness." He reaches out and puts a black disc on the player, moments later the room fills with beautifully relaxing music.

The old man sits back with a slight groan and sits there with a small smile on his face. "Ah, one of Rowena's favourites, Vaughn Williams, the Lark Ascending," he says, as if that means anything to me. Still, you live and learn. I had never heard such a variety of music until I came here, everything had been more upbeat and a lot less relaxing before.

"She always said it was the sanity of her soul, we would go and listen to live music, any music, whenever we could you know. There is nothing as serene as listening to good music being played live. One of life's essentials," he says, closing his eyes and losing himself in the sweet sounds. I hop on his lap, his eyes don't open, but he strokes me ever so gently as we listen to the music, each instrument bringing something special and adding to the story being told. Soon, my eyes are shut and I listen to the music, dreaming. The old man's strokes get slower and slower, until his hand is just gently resting upon my back and I know he is sleeping, lost somewhere in his happy memories, and I slowly glide into a happy and deep sleep myself.

I wake to the click, click, click sound of the end of the album.

I have no idea how long we have slept, but it is warm and comfortable on the old man's lap and he is snoring ever so gently. I am happy to have found him and enjoy his companionship, my life seems richer because of him. I don't want to disturb him, so I just lay there, enjoying the tranquility, dipping in and out of sleep in a blissful state of sheer and utter contentment.

After a while longer, he wakes up and just starts stoking me again as if he had never been asleep. The record is changed and he shuffles off to make himself a cup of coffee. I like the pace here, everything is slow and gentle, it is just a shame everything seems like a bit of a struggle for him. I guess that is what happens when you get old, the pace of life just slows down with the benefit being you have time to enjoy memories — the secret of life must be you just need to make sure you make time whilst you are young enough to make some good ones.

Later in the day, there is a tap at the window and I look up to see a young girl looking in, waving at the old man. "Hello, here she is," says the old man with a smile on his face. He gets up and goes to answer the door.

"Hi Frank, here are your bits. I came a bit sooner as school finished earlier today, thank goodness," she says, laughing, full of energy.

"Thanks Ellie, you're so very kind, our little friend will be very pleased as well," he responds whilst looking at me. The girl sees me and comes over to stroke me. I haven't seen her before, but I don't mind as she obviously knows Frank, who clearly likes her, so she must be nice. "But are you sure it's finished early? Really?"

he asks her, "I wouldn't want you skipping school, it's important you know."

"No, honestly. It's closed this afternoon, the fire alarm kept going off for some reason, so they said we'd have to go home. Brilliant news if you ask me. Probably someone doing it deliberately, but hey ho, haha!"

She sits down in front of the old man's chair. "Anyway, look at these, I took some photos for my coursework. I borrowed a camera from school and then printed them off today. I'm doing a project about different textures in nature, so I was allowed to go to the park and take photos. It's really cool when you have a proper camera and can zoom in, the software at school is great too. You can do anything!"

She gets some pieces of glossy paper out of her school bag and hands them over. The old man takes them and then looks around for something. "They're there," says the girl pointing. He laughs, picks up his glasses and puts them on.

He seems to study the photos for an age, holding them close and examining the detail before moving on to the next, muttering to himself as he does. "These are very good, they really show the textures well. What were they from?" he asks. She proceeds to tell him about how she took pictures of different types and lengths of grass, tree barks, flowers, benches, the path, a fence, all sorts of things. It all sounds terribly dull to me, why take photos of those things and print them off I wonder. The old man seems to have woken up though and is very enthusiastic about them. They chat about the pictures, the camera, the software she used, how she processed them, it is all very technical and I start to get a bit bored, but don't move as it is nice to see them both happy and Frank so absorbed in something. I haven't seen him so animated about anything before, this is a new him.

"You are really very good at this Ellie. You have a great eye and as you learn more, I'm sure you will be able to get a job without any problem. I still know a few people in the business, so I'll call them about jobs if you like?" he says. The smile on the girls face gets even wider and then a slight frown appears. "What else do I need to learn?" she asks. The old man laughs for a bit and then tells her to get some of his photo albums. They talk for ages about photos, moments, lights, exposure, techniques all sorts of things. It may be a bit dull to me, but the girl is completely engrossed and hangs on every word. It is heart warming to see knowledge being passed down the generations, old people can teach the youngsters a thing or two after all.

After a little while longer, I decide it is time I should head home. As normal, I head to the front door and just give it a little scratch; always works. The old man shouts "See you tomorrow!" as the girl lets me out. It is still light, but later than normal and the road is getting busy again, so I should head off. I am a little thirsty after being in the warm room for so long, so have a nice deep refreshing drink of water from the watering can before I go, delicious. I get to the end of the path and just sit in the bush for a bit, the hustle and bustle always takes a bit of getting used to after the tranquillity of Frank's. His place is a real oasis of calm, even better than the park to be honest, but I need both in my life, that's for sure.

Looking down the road, my heart sinks. Black. Bloody hell, what is going on, she's not meant to be around this time of day! But I realise, she probably is, it is just that I am a bit later than normal. I should have gone home earlier, then I wouldn't have to walk past bloody Wilma. It's my own silly fault.

Preparing myself for a fight, as I am sure that is what the meeting will likely result in although it is the last thing I want, I start to cautiously walk home. I have got to get past her to get home, so there is little I can do. Luckily though, she hasn't noticed me and before I get to her, there is a gap in the traffic and she darts across the road, literally a blurred black streak as she is so fast, on her way to the park. She gets to the other side and sits by the fence.

Suddenly, there is a terrifyingly loud screeching sound followed by a metallic crash that makes me literally jump in the air with fright. My attention is drawn in the other direction where I see a motorcycle has just crashed into the side of a car at the junction and the rider has been thrown onto the road. As I watch, a car coming the other way swerves to avoid the rider, mounts the pavement and hits the fence. The noise is horrendous and I jump back into the bush to watch. Luckily, there weren't any people on the pavement, but it is chaos. A car and bike crashed, a rider in the road with people around him now, at least he is moving, and another car smashed into the fence, which looks like it might fall over as it is so buckled and bent where the car hit it. The driver gets out the car, struggling past a big balloon that somehow appeared in front of his seat, no wonder he crashed! How on earth could he see with that thing there? He appears shaken but seemingly okay, he is straight on his phone, so he must be all right.

What could have been a disaster, soon becomes just an inconvenience; no-one was hurt, good.

I look over to where Wilma was, laughing because it must have made her jump out of her skin. Then it hits me, literally like a physical blow, and I feel breathless; the car hit the fence where Wilma was. I can't see her, where is she?

Running over the road, realising too late that I didn't look, I dash into the grass next to the crash site to see if I can see her, fearing the worst. I look, but can't see her under the car or in the area around it either. I start to think I am just being silly and wait for her to attack me, when I see her limping deeper into the longer grass. I can smell blood, she has been hit!

I run after her, through the grass, away from the road, away from the noise. I find her, lying next to a tree in the long grass, on her side, panting heavily, she is covered in blood!

"Wilma, bloody hell, Wilma!" I shout as I go to her side. "Are you okay, what can I do?" She slowly turns to look at me, hardly focusing.

"Oh, it's you" she says weakly, "come to gloat have you? Go on, do your worst. I can't do anything, you've won. I'm done for."

Shocked at her saddening outburst, I reply "Don't be silly Wilma, you'll be okay, we can get some help. Remember you helped me, you looked after me, got me home, made sure I was alright. It'll be all right this time too, you'll see."

"No, you really don't get it do you. We're just cats, no-one really cares about us other than our owners"

"Owners, what do you mean owners?" I ask without thinking; I should be looking after her, not debating.

She rolls her eyes, wincing in pain. "You're so naive, you really don't pay any attention do you?" She winces as she breathes, clearly in pain.

"Stop. What can I do, what shall I do? I want to help you, tell me," I say.

"There's nothing you can do," is her wheezy reply. "I'm hurt, really hurt. That car hit me. I tried to jump out of the way, but it was too quick. It hit me right in my side".

I look closer. "It's not too bad," I say reassuringly, "there's a bit of blood that's all. There'll be bruising, you might have even broken something, but it'll be fine. I thought I was done for when I was hit, thought I wouldn't make it, but I was okay. You will be too."

She laughs, a raspy, croaky, weak laugh. I see blood in her spittle, flowing down her face. "No. I was hit the other side, the side you can see is where I landed. The other side is much worse. I could, I could see bone! It hurts so much."

Tears come to her eyes, they come to mine as well. "Oh

please, stop being so soft," she whispers, "you're such a scaredy cat; always were and always will be. You need to toughen up. You're such a pampered little cat you know."

"I, I know," is all I can reply. "Please be okay, I was, I can help"

"Haha. No, this is it. You were hit by a push bike for heaven's sake. I've been hit by a car. I'm broken, I'm bleeding, I'm... I'm dying." Her eyes close and her face is creased with pain. I wish I could do something, anything. I am lost and don't know what to do. Why doesn't someone come, why doesn't her owner come?

"Stop feeling sorry for yourself" she says. "Get over it, no-one cares, the only person that cares for me is out. No-one even notices us, we're just things in the background to them, animals that come and go, annoying, dispensable. They're all so wrapped up in their lives, they don't see things as we do; well, as I do. I think... I think you're like them. Self centred, uncaring, better than everyone else, it's all about you isn't it? There, you should be happy, you won't be scared witless at night anymore, I won't be crapping in your plant pot ever again, so go home. Go on, leave me, leave me here and get on with your life and be happy I won't be there to bother you again."

I am about to deny that she ever scared me, but then admonish myself, this really isn't the time. "Yeah, you're right about scaring me. You got me every time, every single bloody time," I laugh "good and proper. You're a cow, haha. I don't want to leave you, I want to help. What can I do? Please, I know I was absorbed in my own life, but it's different since my accident, little accident, I'm different. I want to be more like… you. Braver, kinder and a better cat."

"Ha, really," she laughs, or tries to, "if you want to stay and gloat, at least lie next to me, but gently, it's so cold, so very cold." I can see she is shivering, her whole body is shaking even though it is still quite warm. She is in a bad way, I panic.

"No, I'll do something!" I shout.

"What exactly?" she asks. I stand there, looking at my once nemesis dying before my eyes, horrified. She's right, there is nothing I can do, nothing at all. Well, at least I can be here for her, give her warmth, give her some comfort and company, no-one should die alone and drift off into nothingness unnoticed by an uncaring world. As gently and slowly as I can, I lie my body next to her, trying to make as much contact as I can. She winces in pain as I do so.

"Sorry," I say, stopping moving.

"No. Carry on, please," she whispers, "it'll help me. But only stay if you want too."

"Oh, I do, believe me," I respond. "I want to do anything I can. I'm so sorry Wilma."

"What for?" she asks after a coughing fit that causes her considerable pain and results in more blood appearing on her lips and nose. She struggles to get her breath. God, what can I do for her, my poor Wilma?

"I'm sorry for everything," I sob. "Sorry I thought I hated you, sorry I never properly said thank you for helping me, sorry we were never friends, sorry you've been hit, sorry I can't help. I'm just sorry for everything!"

"Oh please" comes the quiet reply, "stop being so dramatic, it's not all about you. I'm the one who's dying you know. Dying alone, outside and leaving Sophie"

"Who's Sophie?" I ask.

"My owner, of course. The sweetest person you can imagine. Loving, kind and oh so funny, but such a tragically sad person deep down. I'm the only one who knows, the only one she opens up to. And now... now, I won't be there for her anymore. She won't even know what's happened. She'll... she'll just think I've just left her of my own free will," she says, crying now with pain and sorrow.

This is breaking my heart, literally breaking my heart. Poor Wilma. "How come you know her name?" I ask. After more coughing and wheezing, Wilma says, "How do you think? I listen! Don't you even know your owners' names?" she asks. Ashamedly, I have to admit I don't, it has never really been anything I have paid attention to. Wilma says she expected nothing else; I'm sorry for another thing now, I can see I need to be better and even more attentive.

"Why does she seem so happy yet is so sad?" I ask. "Poor

thing," is the reply. "She lost her husband, but I never knew him, it was before she got me. Luke, that's her son, never really knew him either. Breaks my heart to see her crying to herself in the evenings when Luke goes to bed. She cries and cries and all I can do is be there and listen; if you listen well, people can open up. It helps them, over time. Just got to be there for people. Care for them, give them the most precious thing we have…"

"What's that?" I ask, "What's the most precious thing we can give?" She laughs, or tries to as another wave of pain hits her. "No, please don't talk," I say, "save your strength."

She's dying and in pain and I am blathering on like an idiot. I need to pull myself together, be there for her.

"Time," she says weakly, resting her head on the floor and closing her eyes.

"Sorry, time? What do you mean?" I ask. I feel I need to keep her talking, it is all I can do. Someone will find us and help if I can keep her going long enough. Please, someone, anyone, please come and help!

"Time," she repeats after a long pause. "Time is the most precious thing we can give, to anybody. Time runs out for all of us… just being there, really being there, when people need us, is the greatest gift we can all give someone else. Sophie needed me, needs me, poor thing. She doesn't tell anyone else how lonely or sad she is. How she's thought about killing herself because the grief hurts so much, How she lives for Luke and not herself really."

"How do you know all this?" I ask. I don't know anything about the people I live with.

"Because I was there for her when she needed me. I listened when she couldn't tell anyone else, but wanted to tell someone who she could trust. And that someone was... That someone was me. I've sat through all the heartache, listened to her beating herself up because she likes the look of some guy, but feels guilty. Poor thing, she needs to move on and find someone and now I won't even be there for her."

"Who does she like?" I ask.

"Some banker type guy. Apparently, he thinks he's the big deal, too flashy for his own good, but Sophie thinks there's something about him. She thinks he's not being himself, like her really. She thinks he just needs a chance. She just needs a chance. I hope she moves on. I'd have loved to see her happy, really happy..." she stops talking.

I fear the worst. Please, someone, anyone help us! I'll do anything, I will be a better cat from now on and stop being such an arse, just please come and help her! Her breaths are getting weaker, I can hardly feel any movement. The clearest sign she is alive is a bubble of snot and blood that keeps moving, albeit slowly, from her nose.

"Please promise me something?" she asks.

My heart leaps, perhaps we will get through this after all, I just need to keep her going long enough for help to arrive. "I'll do anything Wilma, anything, just ask," I reply.

"Look out for Sophie…" is the almost inaudible reply. "Try and make sure she can find me, so she knows I didn't leave her voluntarily. And. Please. Try. And. Make. Her. Happy. Again… she's a… good… person. Please promise," she says, so quietly I can only just hear her now.

I know. Know she has gone. Her chest isn't moving and her body has no warmth, the bubble isn't moving. She is just lying there, another dead animal, another victim, another person taken before their time. Time, yes indeed, that is the most precious thing we have to give.

I gently stand up and look at the still form in front of me. I now understand that she was never a nemesis, just someone who was a bit mischievous, funny I guess, but mostly good. Yes, she had a big heart did Wilma. I can't believe that just as I begin to really know her she has been taken from me.

Tears are flowing freely now. I have never felt so inadequate, so worthless, so absolutely grief stricken. Her last thoughts in life were about someone else, she wasn't complaining or moaning about the unfairness of what happened to her, she was just sad about not being able to help Sophie. Wilma was such a good cat, an amazingly good cat.

"I promise," is all I can think to say as I give her the tiniest and gentlest of kisses on her blood stained head. "Sleep well Wilma, may you have warmth, food and love wherever you are. I'll miss you. I'll do what I can for Sophie and I promise I will be a better cat. Thank you for being there for me and I'm so sorry Wilma, so very sorry"

I'm sobbing and can hardly see through the tears. I give her one final kiss and then head back, into the darkness, Wilma's darkness, towards home.

Clare - Fireworks and Futures

"Please try and be at least a little bit grateful Beau. Come on, I'm bloody trying you know," I say in a raised and frustrated voice at a very sulky teenager who is looking at me with a mixture of anger and disbelief. Perhaps even disappointment? Kids always have a way of getting to you, making you feel as though you are never good enough.

"Yeah, yeah, yeah Mum," is the sarcastic reply that increases in volume to a full on yell, "we all know you're trying, you work hard to do what's right and it's all my fault!" This all started because she told me she needs, really needs mind you, something else now, a camera this time. Of all the things we need, she wants a camera, and not sometime in the future, but right now — all her other needs have been superseded by this one, for now. I am at a loss, she has already got one on her phone, which is why I am paying a bloody fortune each month for a contract on the damned thing, and can get one loaned from school. Money I can't afford, for something I couldn't even justify for myself! Everybody always wants something, but Beau always *needs* everything.

"Don't you dare patronise me Beau, you've no idea what I have to go through. No idea at all. If you want more money, do what I do, get a job! Your friends all have jobs, paper rounds, working at the salon, grocers or the supermarket, that's what they do for spending money. They earn it, ever thought of that? Earn your own bloody money if what I can afford to *give* you isn't enough. Go on, go and find a job, start paying for your own way a bit, give up your time to make some money, rather than always just using your time to spend someone else's."

"Why don't you get it?" she yells back, "I don't want these things, I *need* them. You know, parents *provide* for their kids. Everyone else's parents give them stuff, make the effort. Why do you have to be so bloody stingy all the time? It's so unfair!"

"Unfair?" I say incredulously. "Un-fucking-fair!" she is getting to me now, I hate losing my temper and swearing at her, I love her, but sometimes she just gets under my skin. "I do my absolute best for you, I spend most days looking after people that can't wipe their own arses, all for you!"

"Oh, here we go again!" she shouts back, the neighbours must love this I think again. "You're such a martyr aren't you, it's all about you isn't it? It's not my fault your single, if you hadn't driven Dad away we'd be okay and I've have had a chance. But no, you just drive everyone away don't you, you're so negative!"

Before I say anything else, I just turn my back and go and make a coffee to try and calm down. What can I do, why is nothing ever enough these days? Is it really me, or is Beau just one of life's takers; nothing to give, just after whatever she can get, all without any commitment? I can't believe she still drags up her father, that's low, even for her. No, she is a good kid really, I know that deep down, she just needs time to understand life isn't about getting, but rather giving. I just need to reconnect with her again, life shouldn't be pushing us apart; she needs me, I need her.

I turn around with the steaming cup of instant coffee in my hand. "Come on love, what's the matter, really? You always seem to want things, but nothing ever seems to make you happy. You've even fallen out with most of your friends recently. What's happened? I love you, very much and with all my heart. I want you to be happy, that's all I want. But I can't give you what I can't afford. You know that right?"

That seems to take the wind out of her sails. She was in full flow, ready for another battle of words, another argument. How can she argue when I remind her how much I love her, especially when she knows that's the truth? She closes her mouth and her eyes soften, just a fraction, but it is there nonetheless.

"I love you too Mum…" she hesitates, clearly deciding her next words carefully, will they reignite the conflict or allow us to talk I wonder. "It's hard for both of us. It's just…"

"Just that other people always seem to have more money, more things?" I ask.

"Kind of," she replies. "We've never had money, I know you work hard to provide for us and make our lives happy, but it's just not fair. I know it's wrong of me, but I'd like nice things like everyone else, I'd like to live somewhere nice, go abroad on holiday somewhere nice, have a future, know what I'm going to be when I'm older, meet someone nice."

"I know love. It's not wrong to want everything to be nice, not wrong at all. But the only people that can make that happen is us, you. You are the only person who can really make yourself happy, and that will take time and effort. With a bit of luck, you'll get where you want to be Beau, but it won't happen overnight and I can't do it all for you."

My heart is melting and I walk over and just give her a big cuddle. We don't cuddle enough these days. She responds by melting into me, hugging me tight, just enjoying the moment. She is my baby again, just a girl needing her Mum. God I love her, my poor little Beau. I really should help to give her more of a chance, be there for her more. I may not have money, but I can give her love, unconditional love. Love is free.

"And I've told you about your Dad haven't I. I've no idea where he is these days. I begged him to stay, begged him, not just for me, but for you. I know it's tough not having any contact with him, and that's never what I wanted. He just changed over time, he wasn't the person I met, I've no idea what happened to him.

It was like the good Tom, your Dad, started to melt away and disappear as time went on, slowly at first, so slowly I hardly noticed, but I was losing him nonetheless. He'd been so loving and kind when we first met, he was a real romantic, that's what attracted me to him — and his good looks. We had real fun you know. I loved him Beau, and it broke my heart when he left, even though I knew it was the right thing for me and you."

"You've never said he was romantic before, I never even knew you had a romantic side"

I laugh at that. "That's no surprise my love. How could you

ever know what I was like, what dreams I had and have, what makes me happy, what makes me sad? I know all you've ever known is someone who is your Mum, someone who nags, washes, cleans and cooks, someone that spends most of the time out at work, doing a shit poorly paid job. Someone who can never give you what you want, someone who can never take you on a nice holiday abroad, someone who never dresses up, goes on dates or has fun. You're growing up and just see part of me, the part you know, the part you see.

Don't you the think I was young once, that I had dreams, that I also dreamt of having nice things, a good job, meeting handsome rich men, being happily married, having a happy family? Well, before you say no, I did. I still do. But life takes us in directions we don't want to go sometimes Beau, with or without our help. You realise not everyone will get what they want and sometimes we just get dealt a shit hand. And before you start, I don't mean you. You're the only good thing in my life, I love you."

"Why haven't you ever mentioned this before?" she asks. She is resting on the kitchen worktop, looking at me as if I am a normal human being and not just her Mum for the first time.

"Oh Beau, you're so wrapped up living your life, why would you want to listen to me? I'm just your Mum after all. Why would I want to confuse you anymore by chatting about my innermost hopes or dreams and my frustrations about how they face up to the realities of life? I don't want to make life any harder for you, I want you to have dreams and to achieve your dreams, to be the person you want to be. It's right that part of you despises me, of course you do, you're just worried you'll end up like me and neither of us want that."

"Mum, stop it" she says hugging me again, with tears in her eyes this time. "Of course I don't despise you, how could I? I know you love me and do all you can for me, I love you too. I know it's been hard making ends meet, I can see that, I can see it when you've already left for work before I'm up and back after I'm in bed sometimes. I can see it because you let me have the phone I want while you have a shitty old fashioned one. I know Mum. You're the one who hugs me when I break up with friends and boyfriends, the one who tried to help me with homework, listens to my rants, patches me up when I fall over, makes meals, takes me on holiday when you can, gives me money you can't afford. I know that Mum, I'm so sorry."

I laugh. "Yeah, holidays like good old Broadstairs with its chip eating seagulls. You screamed like a baby when they got your food, but you hated the holiday, we both know that."

She doesn't deny she hated it, but we both laugh about the memory of the seagulls. "So," she says now the mood has lifted after a good laugh, "tell me your dreams then, tell me something I don't know." I protest, but she insists.

"I bet you don't even know my favourite album do you?" I ask.

"You only ever listen to the radio, you don't even stream music," she replies, "so how could I know? You haven't even got any albums."

"Exactly. I haven't got any music now, but that doesn't mean it never used to be important. I used to love listening to music, my Mum had an old record player and she'd always play an album called 'Breakfast at Tiffany's' it was wonderful. You could get lost in the music, which was mainly instrumental, but it was delightful. When I was old enough, I got my boyfriend at the time, Stuart Ellis was his name, a beautiful olive skinned trim and toned boy he was, to take me to the cinema to watch it. It was an old film even then, but mesmerising and oh, so wonderful.

Audrey Hepburn was the star, playing a character called Holly, she was glamorous, a true old fashioned film star. Fun, romantic and beautiful, with amazing clothes and a lifestyle to match. The film was the most wonderful thing I'd ever seen and I dreamt my life would be like that, experiencing different types of love from purely sexual to romantic, having lots of friends, being carefree, having everything just work out and never needing to worry. Just being able to enjoy life, to be wined and dined, to be loved and adored. Of course, when you get older you realise the film was really about the paradox of wanting stability in your life but needing freedom, that's what everyone struggles with really. Do you know, in the film, she has a cat, and it's only ever called Cat because she doesn't believe anyone can own something wild and free, so it never has a name, but she loves it nevertheless.

And even funnier, it's all just about fantasies, because you can't even have breakfast at Tiffany's because it's a jewellers and not a restaurant. But it's wonderful, I loved that film and still do. I'd love to be loved, sexually and romantically, to have fun, not to have any worries, to be like her, Audrey and Holly.

I had flings, good sex, bad sex, fun sex, amazing sex and

meaningless sex when I was younger, of course I did. Oh Beau, do you really think sex is a modern invention for youngsters? Everyone's had sex and most old people have probably had more wilder sex than even you would ever think possible. It's just a fact of life. Adam and the Ants used to sing about it..."

I see I'm losing her, she's never heard of Adam and the Ants and Mum talking about a sex life is clearly too much for her. "Anyway, my point was that it was almost as if that film was written for me; I thought it reflected me and my life would be like that. I'd always wanted to be wined and dined, to have fun, be happy and in love. So, when your Dad came along and didn't want to just get me into bed, but instead wanted to take me on picnics, to plays, concerts, in fact anything and everything, I was smitten. He made me feel like Audrey in the film. He made ME feel beautiful and loved; stability, freedom, sex, romance, I'd got it all you see. But then he changed, he started drinking, taking drugs, gambling, he lost his job, we lost our house, he got violent. Yeah Beau, he even started hitting me, stealing from me, taking from us. It was awful.

Even so, when he left, I begged him to stay. He wasn't himself and I always believed that my good Tom was still in there somewhere; romantic, loving, caring Tom. But, in the end, he went, I begged, but he just went. I never wanted us to be a single parent family, I always wanted you to have a proper family, but sometimes life just doesn't work out Beau and I'm so sorry for that. It broke my heart, as in that single moment, I lost my lover, my dreams, my future and your Dad."

I laugh then as I realise I've been going off at a tangent. "Haha, so, the answer is… Breakfast at Tiffany's is my favourite album. Got there in the end! One day, you'll have to listen to it and watch the film, it's everything that's good and fun about life all caught in a film and an album. Anyway, that's enough about your romantic dreamer of a Mother, what about you my love, what's going through your pretty little head?"

I pause and look at her, I hope I haven't upset her, but it feels good to talk with her. Normally, we just have functional chats and so it feels good to open up a bit. I wonder how she'll respond. She's looking at me in a way she hasn't for a long time, it's a loving affectionate look.

"Mum, I'm sorry. Why haven't you ever told me anything about yourself like that before? That's amazing about the film, the music and that you've had boyfriends other than Dad. I never thought about your life like that. I feel glad you've told me, happy that you had those dreams and everything, but I'm so sad you're living the life you don't deserve. I'd always, always, thought that the way you are was just you. That you just accepted this life because you never wanted or knew of anything better. I'm so sorry I never realised that you don't accept this life, you just put up with it. You put up with it for me. Oh Mum!"

She hugs me again, even tighter than before. She is proper crying now, full on heart wrenching sobs, and I cry too; finally, I have got my girl back. I had always hoped we would be close, but life gets in the way sometimes. We just need to try harder. I will try harder.

"Thanks my darling, that makes me feel so much better. We

need to be more open with each other and start being honest, start planning to get our lives back on track. What do you want to do, after your exams, they're not too far away now? You need to start revising, please don't end up like me."

We sit at the table, she thinks for a moment. "Mum, I want to work in journalism I think, photojournalism. I'm pretty good at it, I'll pass my exams okay. I…"

"Really?" I ask. "You've had some pretty ropey reports from school in the past and they're not easy to pass my love. You need to work at them."

"I know Mum. I don't just sit in my room watching videos all day you know. I do my homework, revise, get on with it. Mr Johnson showed us some good websites to use, so I revise from them. I'm doing okay, I promise. I've fallen out with lots of the old group because they're losers Mum and I don't want to end up like them, like Dad even. I want to work hard, be like what's her face in your film, but be a journalist. I'm looking into options for 6th Form and trying to get a part time job. It'll be okay Mum, trust me."

She laughs as she says the last bit, but I do trust her. An hour ago, we'd been ready to argue away quite happily. Now, she seems ever so grown up and sensible and we seem closer than ever, I couldn't be happier.

"Perhaps we could look into repayment options for this camera you need. But you'll have to help me understand why you need it and what you'd need it for. It won't be the best, but I'm sure we can do something. There's nothing I won't do for you Beau."

"I know Mum, thanks. But I'll use one from school, it'll be fine. I just get carried away sometimes, sorry. I know you do your best. Others may have more money, but I don't know anyone else who talks with their parents the way we just have, and I like it. I want to know more about you Mum, your hopes and dreams and memories. Just, please, leave out all the sex else I'll have to get counselling. Jeez!"

"Deal!" Is all I can manage. I can hardly speak.

"I'll get a Saturday job, hopefully one that'll help me through my A levels, as well. I know I should get one. Things seem clearer lately Mum, it'll be okay. Hey, why don't you think about doing something else, something that'll make you happy? You don't have to do your current job forever, we can both have a brighter future!"

I like the sound of that, but I have no idea how to escape my current job to be honest. I haven't got any real skills and jobs are so hard to come by. Worth a try though I guess, you never know…

Lachrymosity & Promises

Poor Sophie, poor Wilma; it is all so very, very sad. What an absolute nightmare, I still can't believe it. Life goes on as usual for everyone else of course, they are still rushing to work as if nothing has changed, yet in that moment, for us, it did and crushingly so. The crashed car has been removed and, apart from the damage to the fence, you would never know anything really happened. To most people, other than Sophie, Luke and me though, and poor Wilma of course, there was no lasting effect. Just another momentary bit of excitement, a bit of disruption soon forgotten, nothing to see, move along…

But it affected us though, deeply. I still can't sleep properly. I can't stop thinking about her, lying there hurt, dying and in pain. Knowing she was dying, but only worried about her owner, Sophie. You would have thought they were friends, she seemed almost in love with her. I wish I had known Wilma better, there was more depth to her than I could ever have imagined. She knew things I never knew and had an insight into life I had no awareness of. I can't help thinking how shallow my life has been, indeed is. She was a good cat, caring, loving, kind and funny. If only; my life always seems full of ifs and onlys and that needs to change, I need to be more present and in control of my life and care more about those around me.

I sit on the wall and watch Sophie on her steps with the ever present smell of cherry wafting above as she contemplates recent events. Her arm is wrapped lovingly around Luke, but there is no laughter today, only tears and sadness. I don't know how they found Wilma, or what has happened to her body, but I know she knows. I have been to check the site of her passing; I can still see evidence of her rich red life giving blood on the flattened grass where she had laid, I can even sense her and smell her, but she's no longer there. Gone. Vanished from the site of her all to untimely demise, her accidental but devastating death. Gone from my life. Gone from Sophie's life. Gone from life, forever. The fickle finger of fate can be so cruel sometimes. I will miss her and it is clear they miss her too. It hurts my heart to see this mother and son united in their grief, again.

They are just sitting there, looking so sad, lost and alone. It wouldn't be hard for anyone to know something's wrong, if they just looked and had time to care that is. People see them of course, but no one asks what is the matter or whether they can help. No-one seems to want to interrupt their moment of sadness, but if only they would, at least it would show them that they are not alone. Although people don't seem to know or care, it is as though the world itself is mourning Wilma's loss, the sky is overcast and gloomy. This isn't a day to celebrate or be happy and the world seems empty without Wilma.

I observe the well dressed man coming down the road who always seems to notice her without ever really acknowledging her presence. His ever present morning coffee in his pedicured soft hand as he walks down the road with a purposeful stride. I see him looking at them and a frown forming on his face as he nears. She hasn't noticed him, so engrossed is she with Luke and their mutual grief and loss. He slows his step, seemingly unsure what to do. He hesitates at the top of the garden and looks like he will ask her if she is ok, but loses his nerve and doesn't. She hasn't looked up and the moment to intervene has passed, so he picks up his pace and moves on. He walks past, seemingly lost in thought. I watch him walk a little further before he slows and looks like he is about to turn round. I am willing him to come back knowing this must be the man Wilma mentioned.

Please go to her, please, just do it is all I am thinking. But he doesn't, after a moment's hesitation he continues on his way. Shit, so near. I am sure it would have helped, they need someone, any one, to help break their bubble of solitude and sadness, but it is not destined to be him, today. Tomorrow, perhaps.

I feel obliged to try and help. I am not sure what I can do, and am sure I can't really help, but know I should try anyway. It is what Wilma would have wanted and it is the right thing to do. Even I know you should never leave people alone simply because you are unsure what the right thing to do or say is. Give them some contact and a possible lifeline out of their pit of despair.

I get up and hop down the steps, I feel awkward, but I have got to try. I walk to the end of their path, they still haven't looked up, they really are in a world of their own. Why doesn't anyone help, it is so obvious they need a distraction and a friendly face today? I take a deep breath, collect myself, and start to walk down the path towards them.

"Mummy, look," say Luke pointing, "it's Wilma's friend."

Sophie looks up, her sad eyes watching me as I draw near. "Yes, it is, what a lovely cat eh Luke," she says. Undeterred, and being brave for once trying to do the right thing, I walk right up to them and squeeze in between the mother and son. I snuggle right between the two bodies, just lying there, looking at them. I get a stroke from the boy first, and am rewarded by the faintest of smiles appearing on his face, and then his Mum follows. I don't mind, they need the company, I need the company. We have all lost someone very special.

"It's like he knows Wilma's gone to heaven Luke," says Sophie as they continue to stroke me lightly. "I bet they used to have fun together, two friends chasing birds, being naughty and cheeky together, having fun. Wilma was so lucky to have a cat friend living so close, I bet they were the best of friends."

Luke smiles and seems more present now, not much, but slightly drawn out of himself a bit more. We sit there, just the three of us, remembering our friend. We will all miss her, but at least we can be there for each other and share our grief together.

They start talking about Wilma, how she liked Dreamies as a special treat, how she liked having her belly rubbed, how she loved a morning cuddle when she came in, how she was a good cat. She was.

"Do you remember last year at Christmas," says Sophie, "we were just putting the decorations out and you threw some tinsel in the air and it landed right on top of Wilma? She freaked out, haha. She jumped up and tried to shake it off, but it wouldn't budge. She then started to run round the room to get away from it, but it followed her, so she got faster and faster. She was so silly!"

They share a laugh together at the memory, it makes me chuckle too, I wish I had been there to see that, Wilma making herself look foolish for once. We all do at some point, but I had never seen Wilma do anything like that. The memory makes her seem even more likeable.

"And when she would chase elastic bands round the floor," said Luke laughing. "She'd run round and round and round, going faster and faster trying to catch them but never actually getting them. It was so funny Mummy."

"Yes it was Luke, she was such a funny and lovely cat."

They are both stroking me now, almost forgetting I am there as they reminisce about her, and I am glad I made the effort as they both seem a bit happier. It is nice to hear about her life and to listen to them chatting about good times rather than focusing on the loss. I know it will take time for them to fully get over her death, but every little helps as they say. She may be gone, but she is certainly not forgotten.

Suddenly Luke leans over to hug his Mum, almost suffocating me in the middle, and starts crying his eyes out. "I miss her Mummy, it's not fair."

Poor kid, only six and already so familiar with loss and grief, exposed at such an early age to the realities of life. A Dad he never really knew and now his loving cat has gone. God, I feel so sorry for the pair of them.

"I know Luke, I know," she replies quietly, hugging him back and crying softly herself, "so do I. But it's only fair that Daddy gets to spend some time with her isn't it?"

"Really Mummy, do you think they've found each other?" he asks looking up at her.

"Oh, I'm sure of it. Daddy's probably giving Wilma a big cuddle and lots of Dreamies right now and they'll be laughing about all the silly things she did with us. They're together now Luke. It's hard for us, because we miss them both so much, but life moves on and we can only be happy that they're happy. And together. Daddy always wanted a cat, and now he's got one."

"He's got a lovely cat Mummy," says Luke smiling again now.

I can't help but agree. We sit there together for a while longer. I am glad I came over as sometimes it is the smallest of gestures that can help. Sophie's right though, life moves on and we can either fight it and wallow, or try to move on with it. We spend so much of our time either living in the past or the future that we miss the present; but here we are, together, and in this moment I know everything will be OK.

I look up at the grey sky and think of Wilma, I wonder if she is there looking down. If she is, I hope she knows I am doing what I can, as I promised I would. I just need to be there for the Mum and Luke a bit now, put them first. And I know I also need to try and help Sophie move on now as well. Whilst receiving snuggles and strokes from a grieving mother and son, I think on my promise to

Wilma to do what I can for them.

Chance Encounters

Another day snuggling, life is good when you have people to cuddle you. I have been visiting Sophie and Luke every day and am happy that they seem to be coming to terms with their loss. They can't fill the gap in their lives completely, or forget, but then why would they want too? You should never forget the good times and happy memories anyway, all you can hope is that those feelings prevail over the sadness of losing someone precious.

They are a tough couple Sophie and Luke. I like them, they are good people and so good for each other. I just wish I could help Sophie a bit more, but I am not sure what I can do really, other than being there when they need me. Unfortunately, the man that Wilma seemed to think she liked hasn't been back again yet, not that I have seen anyway. I hope they get a chance, a chance to see if they do get on and like each other and to see what happens. What a waste it would be if neither of them ever made the first move, it would be a wasted the opportunity, always so near yet so far. Of course, it may well come to nought, but it is certainly worth trying.

I am running through recent events in my mind as I sit on Frank's warm lap with my tummy nicely filled with tuna, a lovely warm fire in front of us and the sounds of soft crackly music filling the room. He seems a bit more distracted and withdrawn this morning for some reason, but still happy enough. I just sit here enjoying the gentle strokes and companionship too.

"Don't worry about that love," he says to the lady who is spraying some polish into a cloth. "The dust can only ever get to a certain depth you know," he says with a little laugh. "So just leave it, it won't get any deeper now."

"Nonsense Frank," she says, "you've got some lovely things here and they deserve to be sparkly and clean. It won't take me long and I've got a couple of cancellations today, so I can stay a bit longer."

"Don't be silly, you work far too hard. Don't worry about me, I'm fine, go home and relax. You deserve some down time too, please don't fuss about me and put yourself out."

"I won't be long" she says absent-mindedly as she starts polishing. Frank and I watch her, she is like a whirlwind and watching her just makes me feel a bit worn out and glad I can't dust. Picking up ornaments, dusting them down, putting them on the floor and then wiping the surfaces before putting everything lovingly back. She pauses and looks at a black and white photo of some people on a sandy beach somewhere sunny.

"Is this you?" she asks.

She hands the photo over, and after putting on his glasses and peering at the picture for a while Frank replies indeed it is. "Oh haha, I haven't noticed this in years. It must have been taken sometime in the early sixties on the beach in Benghazi in Libya. I stopped off there for a while on my travels and, of all the places, bumped into a chap, oh, Bob someone, who I'd worked with at my first job in Monaco and knew fairly well at the time. It was a beautiful place then, the world was calmer somehow. You listen what's happening there these days and it makes you so sad that everything has gone so awry. I didn't appreciate the place at the time of course, silly really, but that was during my dark period, when I was running from life rather than living it."

"You've had such a wonderful life Frank, you were a real looker weren't you!" she laughs as she puts the picture back down. "I'd have loved to have travelled you know, find all these romantic little places, having fun, being loved, loving life. You're so lucky. I hope my Beau lives life as fully as you rather than being like me."

"You don't need to travel to find romance and have fun love," he says. "It's the person that makes life what it is, not the location, and certainly not the things that people buy. Oh, being somewhere nice can help of course, but the wrong type of person in the right place will have an emptier life that the right person in the wrong location. We've all got to make the most of things. Benghazi was beautiful, but I didn't see that at the time. I was lost without my Rowena, I was blind to life's richness and was lost in my despair."

He pauses for a moment, lost in himself again, then adds "Anyway, if your daughter is anything like you she'll do well in life. Perhaps she just needs a little chance, perhaps just to be a little selfish to get the most from it, but I'm sure she'll be okay."

The lady seems happy with what she has just heard and continues her cleaning, almost dancing round the room as she goes.

Just as the record is being changed to another favourite, there is a tapping at the window. We all look up.

"Ellie!" says Frank

"Beau?" says the lady.

"Huh?" say Frank and I almost in unison.

The lady rushes to answer the door. "Beau, is everything all right my dear, how did you know I was here?" she asks.

"Mum!" says the girl, "what are you doing at Frank's? I haven't done anything wrong if that's what you're thinking, he said I could come round!"

"What are you on about?" the lady replies, "I'm here to look after Frank, I have been looking after him since his fall. He's one of my regular appointments. What are you doing here?"

"Clare, Ellie, what's going on?" says Frank from his chair. I am rather intrigued too.

They both come into the room.

"Hi Frank," says Ellie, or Beau as the lady thinks she's called. "Here are your bits" she says handing over a bag.

"What's that?" asks the lady.

"Tuna and a pack of polos," she responds. Clare looks baffled. "The tuna's for cat and the polos for Frank," the girl adds helpfully. Clare stands there looking confused from Frank to the girl. After a moment, she looks at the girl and says "It's you!"

"What's me Mum? I haven't done anything wrong," replies the girl.

The lady walks over and gives the girl the biggest, warmest of hugs. "You're the budding photographer Frank's told me all about! The girl who saved him from being pushed around by those boys in the park a while ago, the lovely girl who gets him a few bits from the shops and keeps him company!"

"I guess so…" she says rather sheepishly. "And, you're the lovely caring lady who looks after him and will come round even in your own time to make sure he's okay?"

"I guess so…" says the lady rather sheepishly. Then they are both laughing, crying and hugging each other.

Frank and I are still none the wiser. Everything stops as they explain that they are mother and daughter, who have both, unknown to each other, come into this wonderful old man's life. Fate!

It is all rather funny and we are all happy. Clare and Ellie-Beau seem especially pleased. "I was telling Frank how I'd love my daughter to be like his protégé who is talented, lovely and caring," laughs Clare.

"Ha!" she replies. "I told him I wanted my Mum to be as understanding, caring and as kind as the lady who looks after him!" After a moment's hesitation, she then quickly adds "But I didn't really mean it, because I know you are anyway!"

They look at each other and then almost collapse in laughter, with Frank and I just looking on rather bemused.

"So how come I call you Ellie and your Mum calls you Beau then?" asks Frank. I am quite keen to find out too, this all seems very unusual.

"Haha," says Clare, perching on the arm of the chair opposite Frank's, with Ellie, or Beau, snuggled in next to her. I have never known someone to have two names before, it must be very confusing I think. "It's just the silly name I've called her since she was a baby. She used to really love the book Little Beau Peep, she loved the sheep and wanted to be like Beau Peep, she'd squeal and laugh when I read it and make all the baaing noises and then cry whenever we finished the book. She was my Little Beau, and then my Beau. The name just stuck, I've never really thought about it to be honest. I guess she's far too old to be called Beau now."

Ellie-Beau is looking at her Mum, laughing. "No, I love it. It brings back happy memories, reading together, cuddling and pretending you were my sheep."

"Aw, how lovely" says Frank. I must admit to being none the wiser, but everyone else seems to think that has cleared the matter up somehow. I don't always get people, they can be so confusing at times.

"So," says Frank, "this is a lovely little family reunion. My two guardian angels turn out to be from the same family, and neither knew. You couldn't make this up," he laughs, "I should write a book about it. How come neither of you knew?"

"I don't know really," says Clare. "I guess I just get on with work, so I never really talk about it to Beau"

"And I just get on with my life too," says Ellie-Beau. "I'm not going to tell Mum everything I do, she'd only think I was up to no good anyway. Probably think either you were a weirdo Frank or I was trying to rip you off."

Everyone laughs slightly uncomfortably. "Nonsense," says her Mum a bit too quickly. "I'd love to know more about your life and what you're doing. What you want to be."

"I told you," says Ellie-Beau, "a photographer, just like Frank. He's awesome Mum, have you seen his photos?" she says pointing at the sideboard.

"Of course I have dear, I just cleaned them all!" says Clare.

"No Mum, have you really looked? Really looked into them, seen how good they are, who they're of? I'd have thought an old romantic like you would have recognised at least one of the people in them even if you didn't notice the amazing composition, juxtaposition and emotion of the photos themselves. They're remarkable Mum."

"Juxta...proposition indeed, hark at you! Well, as it happens, yes I have thank you," she says picking one up. "Here's Frank in Ben-somewhere with one of his friends."

"What about the princess," says Ellie-Beau, "did you notice her?"

"Princess?" asks Clare "a real princess?"

"Yeah," says Ellie-Beau leaping up, "Frank was Grace Kelly's personal photographer when she got married and became a real princess in, Monaco wasn't it Frank?"

"Indeed it was Monaco," says Frank, looking pleased that she remembered and for the earlier praise. "Those were happy days. I keep that one as it's a real favourite of mine. She was a real lady and a true princess even before she became royalty. I loved her you know, she was such a lovely person. Even after she was royalty and the most famous person on the planet, she still had a down to earth quality that put everyone at their ease. Rowena loved her too. I've got albums of photos from that time in the cupboard. Good times they were. She was another good soul taken before her time. Oh we used to have such fun parties I can tell you, champagne, diamonds and dancing, wonderful they were."

"You're such a dark horse Frank," says Clare holding the photo of Grace Kelly and looking at it. "You're so lucky to have had the opportunity to do that."

"Lucky, yes," he responds, "but you have to make your luck and help it on its way so to speak. I loved photography from the first time I held a camera and realised I could capture moments in a way others couldn't. It's the same as you can give anyone a musical instrument, but it takes someone special to make it sound beautiful. I know that sounds big headed, but I was good, really good — in my day, haha. Ellie is good too you know, she's a natural? She'll make her own luck if she carries on, she's really good Clare. Best eye I've seen in a long time. You've done something right, you should be very proud of yourself! Ellie is a lovely young talented lady, she has a great future."

Clare puts the photo down and sits next to Ellie-Beau again. She gives her an even bigger cuddle than before and I can see there is a tear in her eye. "My Little Beau, the famous photographer, now that will be something! And you've been bringing tuna and bits for Frank since he was attacked have you?"

"Yeah, it was just lucky I saw that dick, sorry, saw Ben and the others pushing Frank around. It just really annoyed me, he's really gone off the rails Mum. I didn't have to do much, but it just felt right to help, so I did. And when we got back, I noticed the photos and we got talking. I've been coming back ever since. Franks a good listener, helps me with my photography assignments and teaches me how to be better."

"Well," says Frank "I can't thank you enough for helping me Ellie. You really were my guardian angel that day, I couldn't not help after that, it was meant to be. Fate brought a budding and talented photographer into my life, just as I am slowing down and finishing my days. It is so nice to be able to have a reason to remember things and pass on a few nuggets that I've learnt along the way, to help where I can." He strokes me, looks at me and then the others with something in his eye, I think it is a tear.

"You three have made me very happy you know. If Rowena and I had been lucky enough to have a family, I couldn't have wished for a better one than you lot. Thank you, you have all helped me in different ways. Cat is my companion, keeping me company throughout the day. Clare, you make me feel so special and I'm lucky to have someone like you that cares about me and spends time with me, makes me feel almost loved again. And you, Ellie, you have given me hope; after everything I read in the papers, you've given me hope that the younger generation are good people and the world will be in safe hands when it's time for them to take the helm. You're kind and gifted and you've given me the opportunity to rediscover some of the things I've learnt and allowed me to pass some of them on. So, from a very old and silly man, thank you!" He raises his cup of tea, his gnarled hands with their swollen joints contrasting with the china mug thats slightly shaking in his hand.

I think we all feel blessed at that moment. Blessed to be part of this special old man's life.

"Thank you Frank," says Clare, "but you don't need to thank any of us, least of all me. You're a good person, and, as you say, it was just meant to be. You've made my life happier and I'm sure you've done the same for the others too." We all nod agreement, well said! "I still can't believe you rubbed shoulders with royalty, that's such a different world to anything I've ever known. Hopefully Beau will have more luck."

"Haha, fat chance of that Mum. I might be lucky enough to get a job I love if I'm very lucky, but we'll have to see about the rest. A long way to go yet though. Anyway, you need to get a new job first," says Ellie-Beau.

"You're leaving?" says Frank, suddenly looking old and slightly afraid, as if by having acknowledged his good fortune it will now evaporate.

"No dear, it's just Beau being silly. I know my lot in life, she's getting carried away. Anyway, you know I love coming round here to see the most glamorous and exciting man I've ever known!"

"You said you wanted a new job though," insist Ellie-Beau. "You told me what a romantic you were, how you wanted more, how you wanted to be like that lady from Breakfast at thingies."

"Breakfast at Tiffany's love. Yes, but life's not like that, that's a dream, just a dream. There's little else I can do and I need the money. It's only having Frank in my life that makes the job bearable," says Clare.

"Ah, Audrey Hepburn. There was another lovely lady, I met her in New York once for a photo shoot. She was delightful, really good fun as well. She had an aura about her, you could almost see it and everyone felt privileged just to be close to her. Gone now of course, I seem to have outlived all the good people, no idea why. Life can be so fickle sometimes. The fickle finger of fate keeps us on our toes though I guess."

Clare is open mouthed at this point. "You met Audrey?" she asks, stunned.

"Yes my dear, just before I lost my Rowena, the year before actually. She was mightily impressed I'd met her, I think she was slightly jealous she couldn't go as well, but it was all organised through Audrey's agents. I think Rowena, bless her, thought I'd lose myself in Audrey's eyes and give her my heart. She was so silly like that. There was never anyone for me other than Rowena, she was my princess, my star. I couldn't have loved her more if I had tried. She was, is, everything to me. She was silly like that though, had a vulnerable side, she never realised just how amazing and beautiful she was.

Anyway, I have still got an album of the photos of Audrey somewhere. I'll dig it out if you'd like? Rowena loved that film though, Breakfast at Tiffany's, I haven't seen it for years now, but it's one of those films that once you've seen it, it affects you and you will always remember. Such an uplifting and lovely film."

"I'd love to see the photos Frank, yes please, I'd love that very much. There's no end to your talents and fame!" says Clare.

"Haha, if only" is his response. He reaches over, gets a record and gives it to Ellie-Beau. "Can you put that on for your Mum please Ellie love?"

Ellie smiles and puts the black vinyl disc on the player. Soft sweet sounds soon fill the room and everyone is listening intently to the words, something about a moon and a river. I love music, especially at Franks, but I can never really understand or remember the words. I think some people can listen to the words and understand the meaning, for me though, they just add to the music, another sound more than anything.

"Do you know," says Frank, "Audrey was so sweet, that she wrote to Henry Mancini, who composed and conducted the music for the film, and told him that a film without music is like an aeroplane without fuel and that his work lifted the film. She called him the hippest of cats. She was just so honestly and utterly sweet. She didn't need to do that, and most big stars wouldn't, they would have just basked in the adoration themselves, thinking the success was solely because of them and forgetting everyone else that actually made it what it was. She was different though, she noticed things as they were, made people feel good, let everyone know how important *they* were. That's what made her a real star more than anything you know."

We listen to the song in companionable silence.

"Ah, here's Something for Cat," he says chuckling to himself. I look up, thinking I am going to get a nibble treat, but there is no food in sight. Frank and Clare both laugh looking at me, Ellie-Beau looks confused.

"Just the name of the song," says her Mum. Oh, funny.

The record finishes and Clare says she is sorry, but she had better get moving as she has got another appointment and doesn't want to be late.

"Don't overdo it Clare," says Frank "and please don't put yourself out coming round later. Just go home and relax."

"What, and miss out on hearing more about royal parties and my favouritest film star ever, no way! You won't be able to keep me away now, sorry," she says laughing. Turning to Ellie-Beau, she says "I'm so proud of you Beau, you've made me so happy. You're a really good person. I'll see you later, okay."

Clare gets up to go, and Ellie-Beau gives her yet another hug. "I'm so proud of you too Mum, you're a really good person. I can't wait to see you later!"

With a kiss for Ellie-Beau and a wave to Frank, Clare rushes out.

"Well, what a turn out for the books," Frank laughs. "You're a lucky girl to have a Mum like that Ellie you know, she really loves you."

"Yeah, I know," she responds.

"Right," says Frank "what would you like to go through today? Oh, before we do though, that piece of paper over there," he says pointing to the sideboard, "that's for you. It's the number of Jimmy Atrill, he's the lead photographer at the City Express. I've known him for years, from when he was just staring out, and I spoke to him about you."

"Me?" asks Ellie-Beau picking the piece of paper up.

"Yes, I've told him how good you are and he says they might have a part time vacancy. I spoke to him yesterday. He's expecting a call from you, so I'd give him a quick call later today if I was you, you've nothing to lose. Remember what I said, we all have to make our luck and give it a little push sometimes. Please Ellie, just believe in yourself as much as I do. Give him a call. Promise?"

"I promise," she replies, giving him hug, "thank you Frank. Thanks very much!"

"Hey, don't thank me yet. I've just told him about you, it's up to you to get the job. Just give it a go, it'll be fine."

After Ellie-Beau puts the number into her phone, she gets some photos out of her bag and they start discussing them. Time for a little snooze methinks!

Peripeteia Al Fresco

Time passes, but it is still to early for the pain to lessen.

We all still miss Wilma, very much, and there is a hole in our lives that cannot easily be filled. I often go and sit by Sophie and Luke now, they have accepted me into their lives, and I rather enjoy their company too.

I am sitting at the top of the stairs, enjoying the morning ritual of clouds of cherry smell wafting over me and engulfing me in their sweet embrace. I am not completely sure whether it is good for me or not to breathe it in, but it certainly smells nice. It is a warm morning and it promises to be another mighty fine day, weather wise. I think I will head into the park and then up to Frank's later, not that I am a creature of routine or anything. I can't help but feel sorry for Sophie though, she is just sat there again with tears in her eyes, I can tell she is reflecting on life and missing those she loved. She seems devoid of hope for herself and she only lights up when Luke is around. Poor little thing, it breaks my heart to see her like this.

She briefly gazes along the road, almost hopefully, but then looks back down after not seeing whatever it was she was looking for. I wonder. Perhaps she was looking out for the coffee drinking young chap in his posh suit, or perhaps unintentionally looking for Wilma, I do every now and again, it is hard to accept she has gone and easy to momentarily forget. It has only been less than a week and I know it will take a while for us all to get over it.

I see him, the coffee cup stuck in his hand as per normal, walking down the road towards us. I wonder if either of them will speak today, it is certainly about time they did. Even I can see they want too, but something inside them both prevents it and neither of them seems willing, or able, to make the first move. Perhaps they simply don't want to appear foolish in case their efforts are rebuffed and they know it will then be awkward every day thereafter when they see each other again. I don't understand them, but I do know that life is too short for missed opportunities though, and Sophie should know that more than most. But, then again, she has certainly had more than her fair share of bad luck and probably just can't see life that way now. She hasn't seen him coming yet. I watch her and will her to look up with all my might, but she is simply so absorbed in her own thoughts today that I doubt she will. I can see him looking at her as he comes, hopefully his resolve will hold firm today and he will finally say something. He is about ten meters away, when it becomes obvious he has lost his nerve, again, as he averts his gaze, takes a sip of his coffee, and starts to pick up the pace to move on by. This won't do and I can't stand to watch this charade anymore.

I might get hurt here, but I need to do something as this is just too painful to watch every day. Without another thought, I rush down the pavement and, just as he is taking another sip of his coffee, I charge through his legs, purposefully crashing into his lower limb as I go, before dashing to Sophie's side.

"Hey, fucking hell!" comes the angry shout behind me. "Bloody stupid cat, I've spilt my bloody coffee all down me now!"

he shouts unthinkingly. Sophie looks up, she is present again.

"Sorry, did you say something?" she says to him.

"Your bloody cat just barged into me and made me spill my coffee," he says, pointing to the coffee stain that runs vertically down his otherwise pristine white shirt. "I'll have to go and change now, and then I'll be late!"

"I hope the dastardly beast didn't take your wallet too," replies Sophie deadpan.

He looks at her intently for a few seconds. "Hey, are you okay?" he asks. "And sorry, that's not even your cat is it, yours is black isn't it?" he says, pointing at me.

"It was black," she replies sadly. "This little fellow," she adds, rubbing my ear, "is next doors. Our..." she stops talking and goes silent, more tears forming in here eyes.

"Sorry, I didn't mean to upset you. The cat just gave me a fright, my fault I spilt the coffee I guess. Are you okay, is there anything I can do?" he walks towards her down the short path, unsure of himself and what to do now he has entered her domain and broken their silent stand-off.

"No, I'm fine. Our cat was run over last week and didn't survive, it hit us both really hard. I'm sorry about your shirt," she says looking directly at him, shielding her eyes from the sun. "You've had a crap enough start to your day without listening to my woes, sorry."

"Oh no, I'm sorry to hear that, that's dreadful news. Awful. I grew up with cats, love them to bits. Anyway, I'm Hector by the way," he says holding out his hand rather formally and awkwardly.

"Hi Hector, I'm Sophie, and if you see a little superhero flying around, that will be my son, Luke," she responds, lightly shaking his hand.

"I live just the other side of the park. I come past here most days actually, I've seen you and your son quite a lot. Not in a weird way though… He looks like a right handful," he says laughing. "Must keep you on your toes I guess, a bundle of bouncing energy."

"Ha, yes, yes he is. Can be a bit of a handful for just me, but we have fun enough, we get by okay."

"Well, I'm really sorry about your cat, and I'm sorry for disturbing you as well. Right, I'd better be off to change my shirt," he says, pointedly staring at me. I wonder if he is actually a cat fan, he certainly doesn't seem to be my fan, but it was a good try though, I will give him credit for that as at least, it got them talking.

"Okay Hector. I'll see you around, I hope your day gets better!" she laughs. They both smile at each other, their eyes locking a moment longer than entirely necessary, before he quickly heads off the way he had originally come from. I detect a certain bounce in his step that hadn't been there before.

"Well done little buddy," Sophie says to me, rubbing my ear again. "Hector seems nice doesn't he? I wonder if he's got some nice young thing to go home to though. I guess I'll never know, he's out of my league that's for sure. Nice to chat to him though eh, rather than never actually getting to speak to him like most other folks round here?"

She continues puffing away on her stick as before, but I detect a slight softening to her features now. Fingers crossed for them, I hope he hasn't got anyone else. They look good together. I also hope Wilma would be proud of me.

"Right!" she says, "time to get Luke ready and get him to school."

She gets up, gives me another stroke and heads in, jokingly shouting to Luke that he will be in biiiiiiiiig trouble if he is not ready in five minutes. She seems happier, good. I leave them to it and head off for my day.

Over the next couple of weeks, I often see Sophie and Hector sharing a few quick words together as he passes by. He seems to be coming a bit earlier these days, almost as if he wants to make time for their chats. Whenever he sees me though, his smile soon disappears and I detect a certain animosity that I wouldn't expect from a true cat lover. I guess I can't blame him for holding a little grudge, but he should be thanking me really. And Wilma of course.

Another couple of weeks pass and life seems to be settling

down a bit. The run of fine weather is improving everyone's spirits and life is good. Hector and Sophie seem to be making each other a bit happier each and every day with their little morning chats, Frank is happy with his adopted family, and Ellie-Beau and Clare seem closer than ever. Especially as Ellie-Beau has got a weekend job at the place Frank arranged for her, she's even taken some photos the paper has used, so everyone is happy.

I am also pleased that Tom and Naomi are also in good spirits, and feel rather proud of myself that I now know the names of the people I share my home with.

A few more weeks and I am rewarded with the sight of Hector sitting on the steps of Sophie's place whispering in her ear, obviously sharing a private joke with her that they are both laughing at. It is lovely to see her truly happy for once. Another time and he is there again and has brought her one of the coffees he always seem to have. She is laughing whilst saying thanks, but that she really doesn't need the expensive artisan coffee as she can make her own inside; she seems to like it though, and they are clearly enjoying each other's company. I even see the three of them on the steps laughing together sometimes, Hector playing with Luke and throwing him around, accompanied by shrill shrieks of young happy laughter from an upside down boy with Sophie looking on, always with a smile and joining the laughter.

I am sat with Sophie late one Saturday morning, when Hector comes by. He is smiling but looking slightly uncomfortable when he arrives with a rucksack on his back. I have never seen him looking so normal before, he has dressed down and is in jeans and a t-shirt today. Sophie notices too.

"Hey, looking mighty casual today," she laughs. "Got time for a coffee?"

"Ooh, I'd love one please Soph," he replies. Giving me a wide berth, and no stroke, he follows her in. Although still detecting a certain frostiness from him, I decide to join them. They are both sat in the kitchen and all seems normal, but I can sense he is feeling awkward as it is a bit too quiet.

"So... I was wondering," he finally says looking at her. "But please do say no if you want..."

"No to what?" she asks.

The floor seems to catch his interest for some reason as he continues. "Umm, well, I was just wondering, and only if you haven't got any other plans of course. Well, just wondering if you and Luke would, err, like to, um, join me for a little picnic in the park for lunch?" He looks up, and sees a beaming smile on Sophie's face.

"Really? Oh, we'd love too! Is that what's in the bag?" she says pointing.

"Yes, I knocked up a few bits and collected a few toys and things, a little rocket thingy and a frisbee. Nothing special. I hope that's okay?"

"You knocked up some food and collected a few bits did you," she says, "just on the off chance?" I think she is teasing him. Even I feel a bit sorry for him now, but not much.

"Well, I, err, bought a few nibbles and bought a few bits for Luke to play with. But please don't feel obliged to come. I understand if you have plans."

"That's so very sweet of you. Thanks Hector, we'd love too. I'll just tell Luke, he'll be so excited. He doesn't get much adult male company, he'll love it. Thank you!" she turns and practically skips out the room.

I see them later in the park. They look like a perfect family; playing, chatting, eating and laughing in the sunshine with a little blanket spread over the grass that is covered in food. It is so nice to see them all happy, they seem made for each other. I watch as Hector tries to teach Luke how to throw a frisbee, albeit rather unsuccessfully by the looks of it. They are happy though, Luke with a big hat and necklace over a football top for some reason, Hector throwing him around, much to their mutual delight, and Sophie tickling Hector, who is also laughing. Perfect.

Hector becomes a regular at Sophie's and they soon become inseparable, a couple who are good for each other. I am surprised one morning when I see Hector leaving Sophie's, giving her a long kiss at the door before heading off, shouting cheerio to Luke as he does. I watch as Sophie admires him as he walks down the road whistling. She sits on the step and starts puffing away, I join her. She is almost purring as much as I am, the change in her is remarkable. It is funny how life can work out, Wilma somehow knew they were made for each other, and how right she was. I snuggle next to Sophie as she sits there, puffing away contentedly, a smile on her face for no other reason than she is loving life.

Months pass and Hector is almost always at Sophie's now, he must have practically moved in. I wonder why he has his own place as he hardly ever seems to be there these days. The summer is a good one, the brown grass testament to the sunny dry days. The park is abuzz with life, a never ending sanctuary of little picnics and gatherings. Laughter, shouting, whooping and chatting fill the air.

I while away my days at Sophie's in the mornings, followed by a trip round the park and then spend the majority of the day at Frank's, who seems happy enough albeit he wheezes a bit more and is slower than ever now. Poor chap, his mind and spirit are young and active, but his body is just a bit tired and feeling its age. Clare is constantly round there, fussing over him and looking after him all hours; she really is just so lovely and sweet. We have seen less of Ellie-Beau now as she is working almost full time at the paper, she's really enjoying herself and when she can come over, she bounds in and tells us all about what she has been up to and proudly shows us her latest photos. That seems to put a bounce back in Frank, he seems to revel in her career; she has certainly got someone rooting for her, he can't get enough of her stories, it must take him back to when he was young I guess. He sits there smiling at her, listening intently and giving advice and guidance when asked for, relieving his youth and being excited about her future. What time he has left, he selflessly gives to others by really listening and paying attention to them.

It is towards the end of the summer that things take a turn for the worse. I am sat with Sophie on her steps, she is wearing a big wooly cardigan as the day has a bit of a chill to it. I saw Hector dash out earlier in the day shouting he would be back as soon as he could. Luke keeps coming out every few minutes, but all she says is Hector isn't back yet. He seems disappointed each time and just goes back inside for a few more minutes.

Sophie says rubs my ear and says, "Not long now, it'll be a lovely surprise you know. I haven't seen it yet, but Hector says it's just what we need. Luke will be so happy." I should be on my way really, I like to keep to my routine, but feel this might well be something worth staying for. I hope he hurries up though, I haven't got all day and Frank will be wondering where I am. He hardly gets out of his comfy chair these days and even when he does he is huffing and puffing the whole time even though he moves at a snail's pace. Clare has started leaving the kitchen window open so I can come and go when she isn't there as he can't manage it these days.

"Luuuuke," shouts Sophie. "Hector's back and he's got a big box!"

Luke runs out excitedly. "What is it, what is it Hector?" he screams excitedly, jumping up and down on the spot.

"Nothing much," says Hector, blandly looking rather nonplussed.

That is weird, why is it such a big box with a ribbon on top then I wonder. I sense something is wrong here, very wrong.

Hector looks up and has a big smile on his face when he shouts "It's only the besets surprise ever, in the whole wide world. Would you like to see... Sophie?"

"No thank you, not if it's nothing interesting thanks," she responds teasingly.

"Please, please, please, let me see!" shrieks Luke, who seems ready to burst with excitement.

"What do you think Mum, should I?" Hector says to Sophie.

"Mmm, I'm not sure. Do you think you should?" she replies. It looks like Luke will pass out if they don't show him soon. I think I will pass out if they don't hurry too!

"Okay. Pull the ribbon, but be gentle," says Hector, kneeling down in front of Luke. He does so, opens the box and screams with delight.

"Can we keep it, can we, please!" he shouts bobbing up and down.

"Yes, he's yours! Say hello to Barney!" says a triumphant Hector.

He puts the box down, puts his hand in and pulls out a little, pure white... kitten!

AAAAAAAAAAHHHHHHHHH!

"He's beautiful!" says Sophie. "Thanks love, you've picked a gorgeous one there, you're so sweet and have such good taste! The latest addition to our beautiful little happy home, hello Barney!" She then disgusts me further by actually kissing the horrible thing.

Oh my days. I can't believe it. How could they?

I slink off to the park to get away from the damn thing and have a good old sulk. No good will come from this I think gloomily. Bloody hell!

Faded Grandeur

I am still far from happy, I feel let down and utterly, utterly, miserable.. How could they? How could they get that damned awful, annoying, dreadful, despicable, little dwarf rat? Honestly, I am speechless, things were going so well, until they got *it*.

The weather is cold again now and there have been strong winds and rain for days. Weather and emotions are so alike, always changing and you don't really know what they will be like from day to day. The leaves have all fallen to the ground and the park feels damp, even on the odd day when it isn't raining. The leaves never dry out and I have to put up with the wet sliminess rubbing against my tummy as I walk round my little sanctuary, there must just be more leaves than normal as the alternative doesn't bear thinking about. However, I have perhaps been over indulging of late, but what chance do I have when everyone wants to feed me now, I can see popularity has a price. The flowers have gone and so too have the people who spent the summer sitting around chatting, laughing and having picnics. Autumn always takes a bit of getting used to, the gloomy chill penetrating bodies and affecting moods. Everything looks busier in the mornings and evening too as the cars and bikes all have lights on, making the world seem more hectic, more aggressive even, with everyone shut up in their cars and houses, or themselves if walking. No-one seems to want to be out and they pay even less attention to those around them than normal, looking down, hunched into warm clothes, desperate to get wherever they need to go.

It is not all bad though. The sunrises and sunsets are beautiful; a real gem to admire in these shortening days, bursts of colour and light that are hidden to me during the warmer seasons. Central heating and fires are another blessing. Apart from Frank's, where the fire seems to be lit all year round, most places don't have the heating on in the summer. There is a certain warmth from a fire that penetrates and calms your soul, which is so much more than the simple heat. I do love just laying and snoozing in the sunshine when it is hot, of course, but it is not the same really. This time of year is altogether more comforting when you are inside, and I like that I can snuggle almost anywhere now and bask in the glow of a fire, or nuzzle up next to a radiator. Heaven.

I start my day by popping round to Sophie and Hector's place. They seem so settled now and he is nearly always there. I have never seen them argue, like the people I share my flat with do on occasion, and they seem to be really besotted with each other. Luke has just taken it in his stride and I even overheard Sophie and Hector discussing how he called him Dad one day without thinking when he was being thrown around and full of giggles. It was a few weeks ago, I had come in just after they had returned from the park and Luke run off laughing to play with the stupid little kitten. They had made a cup of coffee and sat at the kitchen table, I instantly knew that it must be important and was horrified as I didn't get any attention or even a snack.

"Well," started Hector. "That was weird, I'm so sorry about that."

"Don't be silly, it was inevitable it would happen eventually. He's so young and never knew his Father. You've filled that role and done so in a way that makes him adore you."

"I kinda love him too."

"Kind of!" she laughs.

"Okay, I'll admit he's got under my skin, that is a cute good kid you have. But he's not mine is he, he's yours. And Lee's."

"Listen Hex love, don't dwell. I know you feel uncomfortable about the 'D' word, I do too to be honest. Not because you're you and not Lee, Lee will always be his Father, but you are Luke's role model. You *are* his Dad really. It's just a bit soon, that's all isn't it? I don't think he even realised, but I guess unconsciously he *wants* you to be his Dad. There's a permanence with the name isn't there. Dad's are always there, he wants and needs that I think. I just hadn't thought we'd get to this moment quite so soon. It stopped me in my tracks, but the look on your face was a picture!"

She bursts in to laughter and Hector joins in, reaching out and grabbing her hand in his, looking at her intently.

"I'd love it too. Of course I want to be there for him, but I don't want us to be under pressure. God, no-one teaches you how to deal with issues like this do they?"

"No, no they don't. I guess we can either leave it and see what happens, or chat to him about it. It's hard for him too. You're here, but not living here all the time. You're his role model, but not his Dad, you're his Mum's boyfriend, but so much more. He's confused."

"Ha, I'm bloody confused" he replies.

"Me too. But don't worry about it Hex, please. I'm not expecting you to marry me just because he called you Dad whilst in the middle of a giggling fit, upside down and being spun round. No. I love you, and of course I want to be with you forever, but these things take time. We're doing pretty good so far. Oh, bloody hell, I'm worrying now, I don't want you to be scared off," she forces a laugh to hide her uncomfortableness and worry. I sense this is the real worry for her and perhaps a defining moment in their relationship.

"Don't be silly Soph, of course I'm not going to be scared off. I love you too and want to be with you forever as well. I want to be Luke's Dad, if that's what he wants, of course I do and I'm certainly not freaking out over the commitment. I just want to make sure you want me and we'll be fine, together forever, like guinea pigs," he laughs. "I don't want you to think I'm manipulating Luke's affections or trying to worm my way in with yours either. I've no idea what we should do."

"I do," she replies, looking directly in to his blue eyes.

"You do?"

"Yes. We should. Hmm. Yes, we should…"

"What? If you know, say, stop bloody teasing me!"

"We should just do what we have been doing. Keep on going as if nothing happened. We're strong and good together Hex. We're in love and it grows stronger every single day. There's no need to rush anything, we've done pretty bloody well so far. So let's not put any pressure on ourselves, let's see how it goes."

"Good idea brain box. I knew I loved you for a reason!"

"Just my brains eh?" she says laughing and pulling him towards her.

"Well, brains and other things" he laughs, kissing her.

They seem to have got through the last few weeks unscathed as they are still very much loved up. They seem especially happy this morning, Sophie's just been outside, all wrapped up making cherry clouds, and I follow her in. Back to normal, phew; I should get some treats today. Delicious, although I can't fully enjoy them as I half expect *it* to bound in and steal them.

"Brrr, it's so cold today Hex. Winter's almost here," she says.

"You'll freeze out there if you stay out too long. I was worried and about to send Barney out to get you," is Hector's response.

They sit at the table with large mugs of steaming coffee.

"Ooh, thanks love," says Sophie, hands wrapped around the mug protectively.

"Soph, I was, uh, thinking…" says Hector.

"Sounds ominous, another brainwave from Einstein eh!"

"Ha, not exactly. It was about the other week, after the Dgate incident."

"Oh yeah."

"Yeah. You mentioned about needing permanence in our lives. Well, it got me thinking. Don't worry, I'm not about to propose or anything. It's just that, well, it seems silly us over here when my big house is sitting empty just a few hundred meters away. So, well, I was just thinking, and you don't have to of course. But, I was just wondering what your thoughts would be about us all moving and setting up home over there?"

"Home. You said home Hex. Not move house, you mean it, set up our home?"

"Of course. I've never felt so settled and happy as we are. I never realised life could be so good, you know, so happy. I've heard people talk about happiness, but I never really thought it was true. But I believe in it now, because I am! And that's because we have a home together, and I was just wondering about moving our home."

"Well..."

"You don't have to. It was just an idea, perhaps just mull it over and we can decide another time. I'm not trying to take control, it would be our home, all of our home. You wouldn't have to sell here, it would be good to perhaps rent it out, that way you'd never feel dependent on me. You'd have your own safety net in case you got fed up with my cooking. It was just an idea."

"It's not just an idea," she says looking at him seriously. "It's an *amazing* idea! Oh I love you Hex. What a wonderful idea, it'll be fab!"

"Hey, great! I'll look at removals companies so you can get bits moved over, but only when you're ready. We can take as much time as you want."

"I'm ready Hex, let's give it a few weeks. I'm so excited, we'll have more space and be away from the road. It'll be safer for Luke and Barney. Oh, you're a genius!"

Suddenly, Luke rushes in, holding *it*.

"Hey, careful Lukey," says Hector. "Barney's not a toy, you have to be careful or else you'll hurt him. You wouldn't want that would you?"

"Don't worry, I'm always careful!" is the response. "Barney just said he wanted to come and play. With Cat!"

Oh great. Before I can run off, I am pinned to the floor by a silk glove wearing seven year old superhero, and have an over excited Barney placed next to me. On my head to be more precise.

"Aww, see, they're the bestest of friends!" screams an excited Luke. "Look, Barney's kissing Cat."

"Watch it Barney," I say menacingly. "You're going to feel the paws of power if you're not careful"

"Hey, this is so cool. Will you play, please, oooh, let's play," squeals Barney, licking me again. "What shall we play? I know, let's play chase! Come on, it'll be sooooooo much fun."

Barney jumps on my back and starts wrestling me, claws in though, so it is not too bad. He is quite a cute cheeky chap I guess.

"Hey, Luke, come and sit down, Hector's got something to tell you," says Sophie.

When no one's looking, I give Barney a little kiss. "Right little chap, I'm off. See you tomorrow, and look after them!"

I head off to the park on the way to Frank's. I don't hang around as it is too chilly, so not long after leaving Sophie's, I am eating some cold tuna and heading in to the warmth of Frank's cosy little home. Clare's still there. I go in and hop onto his warm lap in front of the fire, he says hello and gives me a lovely rub behind my ear and starts stroking me. He is wheezing more than normal, but still full of life.

"Thanks for the card Frank, you shouldn't have," she says

"It's the least I can do," says Frank, coughing into his handkerchief suddenly. "You shouldn't have come here on your birthday, you must have better things to do."

"As if, chance would be a fine thing," she replies. "Well, I can listen to my new record player of course. That's my treat for later!"

"Oh, that's lovely! You can't beat good old vinyl, with a nice glass of vino to hand. Did you get it for your birthday?"

"Yes! I did!" she almost squeals with delight. "Beau saved up her money from her job and bought me a record player and... the Breakfast at Tiffany's album! How thoughtful is that! Oh Frank, you should have seen me, I was crying so much when I unwrapped it. She shouldn't have spent all that money of course, but wow! It was the best birthday present ever! I'm so lucky." She looks so unbelievably happy, well done Ellie-Beau!

"She's such a lovely kid. That's so sweet and it really is thoughtful of her. Such a good girl. Oh, that reminds me, there's a little something for Ellie in that bag over there," he says pointing to the table.

"Oh really, spare tuna?" says Clare jokingly.

"I think she'll like it as much as Cat does its tuna," he says stroking me. "I spoke to Jimmy, Jimmy Atrill the chap who got Ellie her job, the other day. He called to see how I was. Such a nice chap and it was kind of him to call. Anyway, he was saying how good Ellie is, she's really impressed him you know." He starts coughing again. After catching his breath, he continues. "Yes, he was saying she has a natural gift and he thinks she'll go far, especially as she can just use any camera. She just uses the old ones they have in the store rooms at the moment, but still gets great results."

Clare is beaming, "That's my girl!" she laughs.

"We were just chatting about cameras and he was telling me what she'll be able to do when she moves on and gets one of the new ones for herself. So, anyway, it got me thinking that I'd love to see the results myself. I'm not getting any younger, so rather than wait for her to save up, I asked Jimmy to recommend a good one, with all the necessary accessories, and whether he could get it for me. He was so helpful and chatted me through all the options and models as I'm so out of touch now you see, and we chose one that would keep her going for years. I wrote him a cheque and he got it for me. So that's Ellie's tuna equivalent in the bag, that's her new camera, her very own camera, given with love and hope for a bright future. It looks very complicated, but apparently it's very good, and I'm sure she'll figure it out"

"Frank, she'll be over the moon. Are you sure though? Really, you shouldn't be spending your money like that. I hope she didn't ask you?"

"No, never, she's never mentioned it. I wanted too. Please just take it Clare, it'll make me happy. Tell her the only condition is that she's got to show me the results."

"Thank you Frank. I'm sure she'd want to show you anyway. A photo is just a photo to me."

This sends Frank into another prolonged coughing fit. When he recovers, with Clare rubbing his back and propping him upright with more cushions, he continues.

"Talking of photos, that's for you," he says, pointing to an album on the sideboard. "It's partly for your birthday, but mainly because it's special and I thought you'd appreciate it rather than it just collecting dust."

Intrigued, Clare picks up the album, opens it, then sits down and starts flicking through the pages. "Frank, is this…"

"Yes," he says smiling, "that's the shoot I did for Audrey. I kept the negatives and made my own copy. She thought she had the only ones. Beautiful isn't she? So natural. She brings a sparkle to the images that shines out of the paper. Lovely. Oh, there's also a handwritten note from her at the back, she wrote to thank me for them. Such a nice touch."

"Frank, this is wonderful. Are you sure, this would be worth a fortune these days?"

"Photos are there to be admired, not just sold like commodities. Do you like them?"

"Like them? I love them. Oh Frank, thank you!"

I hope she doesn't get any more surprises today, as I am worried she might pass out.

Clare stays a while longer and then heads off. The room is warm, and Frank and I are soon happily snoozing away in front of the fire. Reluctantly, I head off when Clare comes back later in the day as it is getting dark. I don't hang around and am soon at my place.

The next day, I'm contentedly snoozing with Frank in front of the fire, when there is a tap at the door, and then Ellie bursts in, waking Frank.

"Hey Frank, you made Mum so happy. Audrey Hepburn, wow! She can't get over it. You made her Birthday!"

"No Ellie, you did. That was a very thoughtful present you got her. Did she have anything for you?"

"Yes!" she squeals, getting a camera out of the case from her bag. "Frank, this is amazing! Thank you!" she gives him a hug and is all smiles.

"Jimmy recommended it, he said it would keep you going for a few years."

"More than," she responds. "This is the real deal Frank, top of the range. It's awesome, must have cost a fortune, you shouldn't have, but thank you!"

"Well, there was a condition attached with you getting it you know?"

"Oh yeah, what a tough one!" she laughs. She rummages in her bag and gets an enveloped out, there are photos in it.

"I took these of Mum yesterday at home. That's the record player I got her, and she's looking at the Audrey album you gave her, with some wine as it was her special day. You can see how happy she is from the smile, although it could be the wine you recommended," she says pointing. "I took them with this. Look how far I can zoom in, look at the colours, it's a wonderful camera. I got them printed this morning. It's so cool! They're for you. My little present to you. Look, I took one with the timer of the both of us eating her birthday cake"

"Aww, that's lovely. You both look so happy. Thank you Ellie."

They chat a while longer. Frank's very wheezy and tired, so after a while talking about her job, Ellie says cheerio and tells Frank she will be back tomorrow with some more pictures. It is just the two of us again, with the light noise of the ticking clock in the background and Frank's wheezing to keep us company After a little snooze, Frank puts on another record, he has to struggle as his movements seem more difficult than ever today.

"Rowena's favourite," he says as the soft music starts to fill the room. He looks at the photo of a smiling Calre and Ellie-Beau eating cake and sighs contentedly. "I'm so lucky they came into my life. I'm lucky you came into my life. What more could a silly old man ask for eh?" He puts the picture next to the one of his wife and gives me a rub behind the ear. He smiles.

I'm enjoying the contact, but then he suddenly stops rather than the gradual slow down before we both have a little snooze. I look up at Frank. His face is screwed up and he is clasping his chest, wheezing, gasping and looking as if he is in pain. The pain lasts for a while and then seems to go, I stand up on his lap, something is wrong.

"Hey," he says weakly, stroking me kindly. "It's all right. Everything's all right you know." It doesn't look like it is as he screws his face up again, gasping in pain this time.

I don't know what to do. I go to move, but he strokes me gently. "Please stay," he says. "You're a good cat, you keep me company. Just stay a while longer." He strokes me, so I settle on his lap, but I am looking at him as I do so. He is sweating, it's warm, but not that warm and he usually likes the fire hotter than this.

"I've had a good life," he says weakly. "I'm so lucky you three have been here for me. Life's a funny old thing. I'll look after Clare and Ellie though, don't you worry. Hopefully, they'll look after you too." His face screws up again and he moans in pain, clasping his chest.

The pain fades and he strokes me again. "It's my time you

know, it's been a good innings really. I'll see her soon now, see my Rowena. I've waited so long. So very long, but I'm looking forward to seeing her again, so I can tell her all about you lot…"

There is a tear in his eye now. He reaches over and grabs the photo of his wife. Clasping it to his chest, with the soft music filling the room, he gives me another gentle stroke.

"Thank you old friend," he says almost inaudibly. "I'm sorry, but I've got an appointment to keep, with a beautiful lady."

He smiles whilst looking at the picture of Clare and Ellie-Beau, holding his wife's picture to his heart and gently stroking me ever so slowly. His hand stops, he quietly gasps, shudders, and then remains still.

I listen and watch, but nothing. I know. I know he has gone. Eyes that have seen the light of over thirty thousand days will see no more. I can't believe it, yet it is not a complete surprise and it is not the same as when Wilma died with such unexpectedness, but another hole burst into in my heart nonetheless. Another good person at eternal rest. I sit for a while, tears flowing. But then I look at Frank and see there is the barest of smiles on his face, he is happy and at peace. I look at the picture of his wife and know why. They are together, again.

Sleep well Frank, sleep well dear Frank.

Round and Round and Round We Go

Weeks pass and the weather is mostly stormy, fitting my mood. Life can be cruel, taking those we love and discarding us to carry on alone with just our thoughts and memories. It is no wonder people can seem so sad and self centred sometimes, life can be so harsh and unfair sometimes, and of that there is no doubt.

I was there to see Frank leave on his final journey, the eternal adventurer finally setting off on his last trip. It was so utterly heartbreaking. I had gone to his house as I was unsure what else to do. Clare and Ellie-Beau were both there, crying and looking absolutely devastated. A long black car arrived, with windows along its length and a long dark wooden box in the back covered in flowers. Clare and Ellie-Beau were dressed in black and another dark car arrived, both parked in front of the house as life continued rushing by around them. Some people glanced out of interest, some with a look of understanding on their faces, but most just looking at the inconvenience caused by the parked vehicles out of curiosity. I had walked up the path just before they came out, mother and daughter holding hands, joined in their grief.

They saw me sitting by the door. Clare smiled and said it was right I was there and Frank would have liked that. Whilst she bent down to rub my ear, Ellie-Beau ran back in, coming out a moment later with a bowl of tuna.

"Frank would approve love," said Clare. He would, he was

such a kind gentle hearted person. With a final rub of my ear, they lock the door, hold hands and walk to get into the rear car and follow Frank off on his last journey. I saw them crying in the back, seeking solace in each other's company, both joined in shared grief. I hoped they would be okay. Once the cars turned the corner, I ate the tuna and then sat there and remembered one of the kindest loveliest people I had ever known. I guessed this would be the last time I would be here like this as someone new would probably live there and it would never be the same again. Life moves on and doesn't stop for anyone or anything.

How can I move on though? Everything changes, some are good whilst others seem senseless and leave a hole in my life. I guess it is the same for everyone, but change affects us all differently and we need to find our own coping strategies.

After a morning walk round the park, chilly as ever, I feel lonely as I get to Frank's again. I stand on the path of his garden. No tuna, no light, no expectation of a warm fire, soft lap, company, laughter, loving strokes or sweet music. All I see is an empty shell of a house, curtains drawn. Soulless, the home has been turned into a house and those days have gone. Forever.

I decide to see if Sophie and Hector are in. I am nearly there when my heart catches in my throat.

"Stop, stop!" I yell at the top of my voice.

I run, driven by panic to be faster than my out of condition body would normally allow, getting there just in time to barge Barney away from the road just before a bus rushes past, causing our fur to billow in its wake. Barney is outside, by himself! I push him away from the road and we sit under the bush together by the wall. We are both shaking with shock.

"What were you thinking of!" I shout at Barney, who is clearly shocked and looking skittish. "That was so stupid, you could have gotten yourself killed! This is a dangerous road, this is where Wilma died. Never, ever do that again! What were you thinking of?"

"I just had to get out, they're driving me crazy!" he replies as if that justifies his actions. "They're all acting a bit strange today, Sophie even got cross and shouted at Luke. There are boxes everywhere, and they get really cross whenever I try and sit in them, as if I can help it! They have been shouting at me and I even thought they might even try to hit me at one stage. Just because I love boxes!"

· "Haha, that's not just you, everyone does," I laugh, "they're like magnets aren't they? They're tantalisingly exciting, safe, and rather comfortable too. That does seem very mean. What's going on I wonder?"

"I don't know. They're all just stressy today. The boxes were delivered a couple of days go and that's when it all started, but it's just worse today. They even tried to stop me from going in the garden. It's just not right!"

"No, that is weird. I wonder why they're being like that? But it's no reason to try and get yourself killed. That bus would have hit you, you'd be a squashed mess on the floor if I hadn't have stopped you, you need to remember that no one else cares about us and most people don't even see us. The bus would have probably just carried on. They're all just in a rush, wrapped up in their own lives. Do you understand Barney? It's important! You could have died just now! Would you want that? You'd be gone, and Sophie and your family would be devastated. You can't do that to them, or me, you need to be careful!"

"Yeah yeah, I know, I know" he responds, getting over the shock and being a bit cocky again. "I just wanted to go to the park, to get away, have some space. That's all."

"I get it, but bloody hell, running in front of a bus isn't going to help anyone is it?"

"No," comes the meek reply.

We nip behind the bush where it feels a bit safer and spend a while watching the people, bikes and cars rush by as I talk him through crossing the road safely; what times of days are safest, what you must do, what to look for, when you move, when you don't. Bless him, when he stops being cocky and silly, he really takes it in; he is a quick learner.

After a while the traffic is much quieter, so I cross the road and wait in the bush on the other side and wait for him to come over, under supervision.

"Good, well done. Don't forget what we've discussed in the future, it would be such a waste if you got run over."

He looks at me, pleased as punch. "Aww, I never knew you cared about me so much," he teases.

"Shut up you fooool," I respond, adding more light heartedly, "I'm only thinking about Sophie and Luke you know. Couldn't care less about you."

He sticks his little pink tongue out in reply and we both laugh. The day has brightened up and I momentarily forget my woes as I show Barney the delights of the park. He is exhausting, he literally wants to go everywhere, see everything and climb anything he can. It is nice though to be able to pass on my knowledge to him and it makes me think of Frank. My moment of reflection is short lived as Barney barges past me after a squirrel that darts up a tree with him trying to follow unsuccessfully. He makes me laugh.

"What's wrong?" he asks. We have just crossed back over the road and I have stopped in Frank's garden. I sit there, looking at the empty shell that was a home.

"Oh, nothing," I say. "Just thinking of life and remembering happy times. The meandering river of life is simply..."

"Hey, want to race home?" he shouts, having not been listening to me at all. "See you there slow coach!" As simply as that, life moves on. I smile, roll my eyes, and bound after him, I am sure I can feel my belly unseemly swaying underneath me as I do so. There's no chance of catching him, but I give it a go, just to make it more fun for him.

There is a big lorry outside of Sophie's, parked half on the pavement, surrounded by little cones. A couple of men I have never seen are walking up a ramp carrying cardboard boxes into the cavernous interior. It is full of stuff, Sophie's stuff...

"Here he is! Got him Soph, Barney's back," Hector shouts when he sees Barney and scoops him up. Barney doesn't even have time to gloat about beating me. He is taken straight inside and the door is shut, in my face. Nice!

I hope he isn't in trouble, but I don't think so. I can't quite understand what is going on though, it's still all very strange. Not sure what to do, I glumly walk up to my place, find a sheltered spot on the terrace and observe the comings and goings. The men keep going in and out of the flat and putting things in the back of the lorry. There is no sight of Barney, but Hector and Sophie keep coming out to look in the back. Eventually, the ramp is removed, placed in the back of the lorry and the doors closed.

"Thanks chaps," I overhear Hector saying to the men. "Good job, that didn't take long at all."

According to the response they are professionals apparently. Professional box and furniture carriers, never heard of it before. Hector continues, "Righto, so we'll see you at our new place tomorrow, but everything that's been marked goes in to storage first. Okay?"

Apparently everything is fine, understood and all agreed. Moments later, the lorry sets off with a double beep from its horn.

Hector and Sophie are stood there watching it go and embrace each other. To me, she seems happy and sad in equal measures and I can't quite figure out what is going on.

"Oh, I hope we're doing the right thing Hex. It's all seemed to have happened so fast now the times come."

"It'll be fine love," he replies, pulling her towards him and giving her a soft kiss on her forehead. "It's the right thing to do, we all agreed it's for the best. Hey, we're going to have a wonderful life in our new home. Trust me, I'm a banker haha!"

"I do," she replies with a tear in her eye, but a smile on her face.

"Right, let's get Silly and Billy and then we can get going. Must be the closest move ever!" he laughs. They go inside and moments later come back out holding hands with Luke on one side and Barney on the other, in some kind of box with a handle on top and a cage at the ends.

"Lets go, yeah," I hear Hector shout as he leads Luke away from me. Sophie, with Barney in the box, turns round and looks at her place and then follows the others. From the box, I see a sad little white face looking up at me as they go.

I dash down and look in their window, the place is empty. They have taken everything, moved it all and gone. I realise that I have just lost Barney! They've gone, they have all gone and I didn't even get chance to say goodbye. Everyone's leaving me these days and I feel hollow and alone; I am by myself again.

The next few weeks are really tough. The biting winds of winter blow the last of the leaves around the damp park, just to make things seem even more desolate. Dark days with more gloom than light. Memories, that is all I seem to have now. I walk round hardly looking at anything, in default mode again, existing rather than living. No Frank, no Ellie-Beau, no Sophie, Hector, Luke or Barney, no-one. I did see Clare once, but she cycled past without seeing me as she was looking down rather than face the biting wind. I visit the old haunts every now and again, but they are all just empty shells, lives that were, distant memories now. I had a wonderful life which had been enriched by wonderful friends, but in the blink of an eye, they have all gone and it is just me left, all by myself. I have Tom and Naomi, or my owners as Wilma would have called them, but it is not the same, nothing is anymore.

The first change that affects me happens one overcast day when another lorry turns up at Sophie's. I hear it and rush to the terrace steps and watch expectantly for the men to put Sophie's things back, so I can start rebuilding my life. But there is nothing familiar in the items they put in the flat and the people aren't known to me either. Not old, not young, just a man and a lady of middle age. I see the man drive off and I start hoping that maybe they will be nice and I will be able to pop round for nibbles now and again, to have places to go for company. My hopes are shattered when the man pulls up outside again and I see *it* in the window. *Its* stupid looking moronic face is pressed against the window, tongue lolling out and ears flopping. Bloody hell! They've got a shitting dog!! Oh my days! This is far too much for me and so I sulkily slink back inside, in an even fouler mood that I would have thought possible, that place is off limits for good now and my world continues to shrink.

I'm starting to think I am cursed to have a solitary life, surely nothing else can go wrong…

I wander around the park the next day, still in a miserable mood and all alone with my dark thoughts, sulking about the dog I heard yapping away this morning. Not only is my life emptier now, but it is also less fun. The last thing I need in my life is to hear that miserable mutt night and day. How could Sophie have done this to me? I helped her in her moment of need after all, I was there for her and this is how she repays me! I start considering that perhaps an unintended consequence of helping her to be happy means that I will always be sad; if so, I decide it was worth it. That thought makes me feel happier in itself, which is a bit of a paradox and so I decide it is too much effort to contemplate further.

The park is quiet; cold, damp, dark and just about devoid of life, whether that be human, animal or vegetation. Utterly bloody miserable. I decide to keep my spirits up and meander over to the western side, near the big houses with the quieter road.

It can't be, my eyes are kidding me, surely. Is it? No, impossible. Hang on, it is!

"Barney, Barney!" I shout, running over to the even bigger bundle of white fluff than I had last seen a few weeks ago. He turns, it is him!

"Barney, where did you come from? Are you okay? How did you get here? Are you lost? Where…"

"Hey, hiya. Yeah, I'm fine thanks," he says. "We all are, we were wondering when we'd see you. It's been ages. What took you so long and why didn't you pop over sooner? I thought I must have annoyed you somehow."

"What do you mean, who's we and why were you expecting me? You moved, left me, where did you go and how come you're back?"

"Haha, we didn't leave. Well, we didn't go very far. We only moved there" he says, looking at one of the large houses. "We only moved round the corner! How cool is that? It's bigger, has a lovely back garden that's nice and safe and it's easier to get to the park too."

"Sounds great. I've missed you all and thought you'd gone for good! How come you moved here? And how come I haven't seen you before now, have you been hiding?" I ask, although it doesn't really matter, I have found them!

"It's Hector's house, he always had it."

"Ahh, now I remember, silly me, I saw him here once before. I knew I'd seen him round here, but I forgot."

"Yeah. And after we moved, I was put in a cat hotel for a week and they went on holiday. I think it must have been somewhere sunny as they're all very tanned."

"Lucky them" I reply; that is what I need, sunshine.

"When they picked me up, I wasn't allowed out for ages. I heard them talking about it and they said they were worried I'd go to the old place and get lost if I went out. As if! But I'm allowed out whenever I want now, I've even got my own little door. It's so posh. Come and see, come in!" With that, he dashes off and I follow him towards the big posh house.

We go through a little flap in the back door. What a nice place, it is big, clean and homely. It has a certain familiarity as it has some of Sophie's things, but most are new.

"Mum, Look! Barney's friend's here. You said it would. Yay!" shouts a necklace accessorised football kit wearing kid. Luke!

"Hey, hello stranger," says Sophie. She rubs my ear and gives me some treats. At last, things are looking up.

"Oh, him again," says Hector as he comes in. He sounds cross and I start to think he still bears a grudge, but then he smiles and rubs my ear too.

I spend a while at Sophie's with Barney, and then head off home. I feel so much happier, my world has expanded again, just a tad, but the feeling of having friends in my life again is wonderful. I become a regular at Sophie's again. It is not a first thing in the morning visit, but I like to fit them in mid to late morning if I can.

Barney and I become firm friends, he has turned out all right.

The weather starts to warm up again, the leaves bud, blossom blooms and the flowers grow. Life picks up, in every way and I feel free after the confinement of the dark winter. Spring is a time of fresh starts, a time for hope, and warmth.

I am just heading home after having been at Sophie's when I notice a van outside Frank's old place. Some men are taking some furniture in. I feel a bit sad seeing it, but at least I didn't have to witness his things moving out and time does move on. I am sure he would have wanted someone to enjoy the place rather than it being left empty and then to become derelict. I just hope they don't have another dog, one nearby is bad enough.

A few days later, I see the front door of Frank's old place open. Intrigued, I cautiously sniff the air for dog smells and then head into the garden to see if I can have a little peek inside to see who has moved in. It must be another old person I think as I see Clare in the doorway.

"Hello beautiful," she says, walking over and stroking my back. "Come to welcome us into our new home have you? Isn't it wonderful!"

Your new home?

"Beau, Beau, we've got a full house again! You'd better bring the celebratory meal out for our little friend," shouts Clare looking back into the house.

A moment later, Ellie-Beau comes out with a bowl of tuna. "There you go," she says placing it down. "I'm sure this is the only reason Frank left you everything Mum, so you could look after this little chap."

After having eaten, I go inside. As I enter, I see that much has changed, mainly that it is cleaner, newer and fresher. Some things are comfortingly familiar though, the record player on the side with an assortment of Frank's albums next to it, and some photos on the shelves, but most things are new. There is a new television, new furniture and a new carpet.

I am not sure where to sit, unfortunately the fire isn't lit, which is another change as it used to be constantly alight. I am scooped up and Clare holds me and gives my ear a rub. She walks with me to the sideboard where the photos are.

"What a lovely man he was, wasn't he Cat, he may have gone, but he's still here with us really. That's our Frank there, next to his wife, Rowena. Over here, we've got royalty and stars with Princess Grace and Audrey, what an amazing collection, and a lovely way to remember our guardian angel. He left us everything, the whole lot! House, savings, photos, records, everything! We are so very lucky that he came into our life, I felt so guilty when I found out what he'd done, but when I recovered I simply cried at the sweetness and thoughtfulness of him. So, you're welcome here whenever you want little chap. You're part of our family whenever you want, and they'll always be fresh tuna!"

I like the sound of that! Good old Frank.

"Mum, he can't understand you you know! It's just a cat," says Ellie-Beau standing next to her Mum. "Right, I'd better be off, we're off to the football ground today, they're teaching me sports photography now. How cool is that! Any plans?"

"That is very cool love, about time they got more women involved with sports, you will be great at it. Oh, nothing much, just doing a bit of house work and then I'm off to college. It's going quite well really, I've always wanted to do something different. Frank's kindness has changed everything, we've now got stability, a beautiful home of our own and enough money to have a future that will let me do what I want rather than having to simply get by and survive."

"Good for you Mum, you'll be a natural at garden design. That's exactly what Frank would have hoped for. We've both got bright futures ahead of us now, all because of him. Chelsea flower show next year then!" she laughs as she lightly punches her mum's arm.

"Ha, we'll see. One step at a time!"

I couldn't be happier. Apart from Frank and Wilma, my life is complete once more. I have a world, a safe and happy world where I have companionship, routine, purpose and love. My days are filled with walks round the park, house calls, nibbles, strokes and happiness. The only thing that is suffering is my tummy, it is getting so embarrassingly wobbly now that I may have to start watching what I eat soon, but not yet, that can wait for another day.

Life moves on. Sometimes we can control the direction, and at others we are simply passengers, having no say in our destination. We have to take the knocks and get through the tough times, but also have a duty to make the most of the good times when they come. Be present and live, make time for friends, have fun and be conscious; never, ever, waste a moment and squeeze every bit of happiness out of it you can.

As a wise old man once said, may you be lucky, but don't forget to make your own luck and help it on its way sometimes.

<u>Life Goes On</u>

Mmm, perfect! Just lying here, basking in the warmth of the summer sunshine, the heat caressing my freshly re-toned athletic body as I relax into a soft and comfortable lap and listen to Larks Ascending softly playing in the background. I never used to really appreciate these moments, but I do now. I luxuriate in the warmth, the comfort, the sheer joy of the moment, having companionship, being stroked, being loved, feeling loved, and loving. I purr contentedly and enjoy being present in the moment.

I am far more active now than I used to be. I used to kid myself about how I looked and my abilities. But I am different now; I am a realist, I am conscious and aware and never, ever, think I'm more than I am. Life is good enough as it is, just being me, there's no need to embellish nowadays. But exercise has made me stronger, faster and fitter than ever before and I have been able to cut down on my food too as I have willpower and focus. I'm in my prime, even being my normal modest self, I can't deny I am in great shape. I must admit that whilst I'm also not fussy any more, I did thoroughly enjoy the big bowl of what I overheard to be fresh, line caught, sustainable tuna, all washed down with tasty watering can water. Yum, life is good!

I stretch my powerful limbs, careful not to catch the old man on my razor sharp claws as I don't want to tear his paper thin skin, and am enjoying the sensation of muscles relaxing in the warmth and softness of the old man's lap. He's so lovely and kind. I adore him; I love listening to his stories, being stroked, indulging in our togetherness, listening to his music and enjoying each other's company. I am made for this life and deserve it, the warm rays of light pass through my closed eyelids as I relax. Perhaps I should have a quick snooze while I bask in the loveliness of the moment — just a quick cheeky nap.

Tap, tap, tap.

Hey, what the hell is that noise and who is making it? It's normally just silent here, apart from the ever present soft methodical ticking of the clock, the sound of soft sweet music and contented sighs. I wish they would just go away, they shouldn't be allowed to spoil my moment, I'll ignore them, I'm sure they'll stop and go away, I deserve this moment of comfort.

Tap, tap, tap.

No, no, NO! Come on, you'll wake the old man up as well soon. Leave us alone, we deserve our peace and quiet after another hectic day doing good.

Tap, tap, tap.

Suddenly, I sense a presence, something is wrong, very wrong. A moment later, I can hear scraping — a long slow nails-on-a-chalkboard type screeching, eery, loud and... close. This seems all too familiar, but the sleepy fogginess of my mind won't allow me to make the connection. Eyes reluctantly prise open and I am instantly on alert, the dream has gone, drifted away like the ending of Shostakovich's violin concerto. The room is dark with just the soft glow from a streetlight lazily shining through, creating pools of light contrasting against the darkness and the shadows.

Hairs rise, pulse quickens, muscles tense, senses are alert. This isn't right, no-one and nothing should be here, it's the middle of the night and everyone is sleeping, or should be.

I feel a presence. Without looking up, I know there is a killer watching me, readying to strike, about to pounce and rip a gaping hole in my throat. Why me? This shouldn't happen to me, I am not an animal, I'm civilised and live in a civilised world. It may not be perfect, I might even have the odd minor flaw, but this just shouldn't happen. Not to me. Life has many cruel twists. I shut my eyes for two seconds and it has found me, I should have been more careful, more aware.

Too late now though, the moment is here. It has selected me as its prey, whether deliberately or not, it doesn't matter. The time has come, my time has finally come. I'm undecided what I should do, the killer in me, the raw animal killer I usually suppress, wants to fight. Fight and kill. The civilised side of me wants to flee, avoid violence at any cost; run, hide, get away. I know that is not an option though, not now, there is no escape. The cat in me wants to freeze, just go back to sleep, dream happy thoughts and hope for the best. Even that's not an option though, it is far too cold and, because I'm getting on a bit now, I need to use the litter tray the people I share with the flat have just got me. A couple of midnight accidents on the floor and it appeared, straight after Tom stood in my little puddle one morning, to his obvious delight. Age affects bladders for some reason, I wonder why. No, I need to focus, I realise I need to fight. So be it!

Decision made, I feel much better, I can feel my powerful limbs waking, blood flowing, muscles charging and readying for what must be. I listen, the scraping has stopped, I know it's watching me, it has sensed that I am awake and is also readying itself for the violence to come, enjoying the pre-fight excitement, probably drooling at the thought of eating my magnificent flesh.

With one last minute stretch, I am ready. My senses are fully alert now and muscles primed because violence it must be, a fight to the death. Slowly, ever so slowly, I raise my head by the smallest fraction, just enough to increase my field of vision, and have one last look before I must act. Any advantage I can give myself, however small, might make the difference. My eyes raise in to the darkness, eyes filled with fury and hate stare back, already watching me, knowing they have found their prey, violence shining from them like sparkles from diamonds, evilness personified.

Anger , raw animal anger, courses through my veins and I leap from the sofa, leaving the relative warmth of my slumber. My muscles are taught and powerful, my teeth are strong and sharp, my claws sharper; my tummy wobbles and my back may ache a bit, but there's still fight in the old cat yet. Our eyes meet, they are wide and surprised, you weren't expecting your quarry to be more barbaric than you! I fly through the air, the tension has been released, I am not just ready for this, I live for this!

I skid to a halt, realising the windows and door are shut tight. We glare at each other, if only there was a way to get to you, I would rip you from limb to limb; it would be a fight of the titans, a fight to the death. I'd taste your blood, drink your fear. I would, if only I could get to you.

The beast raises its head fully into the light, sensing victory, in no rush.

White fluffy fur comes into view. And a big happy smily face.

Tap, tap, tap.

The screeching noise again as the claws move down the window. Not again!

"BARNEEEEEEY! You little shit," I laugh. "You wait, it's not funny you know, not funny at all. Not at my age, especially with my weak bladder! I'll get you, it might be later in the morning, after a little snooze and some food, but I'll get you. Don't you worry, you'll be sorry."

Barney, how did he know? It's been ages since anyone's done this to me. Cheeky little bugger! At least he hasn't… "Hey, hey. Don't you dare, that will smell you know."

He looks at me and laughs at his little tribute to Wilma. He turns his back and slowly heads off down the stairs to the sound of the new bloody dog yapping away. I smile as he disappears and head off to my warm spot on the sofa, via the litter tray.

Time to dream of being with Frank again; one day my friend, one day soon.

May you be well, may you be happy.

<u>The End</u>

Printed in Great Britain
by Amazon